INNOCENCIA
A story of the prairie regions of Brazil

Alfredo d'Escragnolle Taunay,
Viscount of Taunay

(Under the pseudonym "Sylvio Dinarte")

Translated from the Portuguese and illustrated by
James W. Wells, F.R.G.S.
CORRESP. MEMB. GEOG. SOC. OF RIO DE JANEIRO

Originally published: LONDON, CHAPMAN AND HALL, 1889.

ISBN-10: 1541120647

ISBN-13: 978-1541120648

Cover: *A Morpho menelaus while resting,* by Derkarts. Wikimedia Commons.

Contents

THE TRANSLATOR'S PREFACE..5

CHAPTER I: THE SERTÃO AND THE SERTANEJO.............9

CHAPTER II: THE TRAVELLER..21

CHAPTER III: THE DOCTOR...34

CHAPTER IV: THE HOME OF THE MINEIRO......................41

CHAPTER V: THE PRECAUTION..49

CHAPTER VI: INNOCENCIA..55

CHAPTER VII: THE NATURALIST.......................................63

CHAPTER VIII: THE MIDNIGHT GUESTS...........................68

CHAPTER IX: THE REMEDY...76

CHAPTER X: THE LETTER OF RECOMMENDATION........81

CHAPTER XI: THE BREAKFAST...93

CHAPTER XII: THE PRESENTATION..................................99

CHAPTER XIII: SUSPICIONS...104

CHAPTER XIV: REALITY..111

CHAPTER XV: THE ADVENTURES OF MEYER...............121

CHAPTER XVI: THE DYSPEPTIC PATIENT..................129

CHAPTER XVII: THE LEPER..142

CHAPTER XVIII: BITTERS AND SWEETS........................148

CHAPTER XIX: HOPES AND FEARS..................................158

CHAPTER XX: FRESH ANECDOTES OF MEYER............165

CHAPTER XXI: THE PAPILIO INNOCENTIA....................171

CHAPTER XXII: MEYER DEPARTS...................................175

CHAPTER XXIII: THE LAST INTERVIEW........................182

CHAPTER XXIV: THE TOWN OF SANT'ANNA................192

CHAPTER XXV: THE JOURNEY..201

CHAPTER XXVI: A CORDIAL RECEPTION......................206

CHAPTER XXVII: HUNTING THE DOE............................210

CHAPTER XXVIII: IN THE HOUSE OF CESARIO............216

CHAPTER XXIX: THE DOE AT BAY..................................227

CHAPTER XXX: TOO LATE..236

EPILOGUE: MEYER REAPPEARS......................................244

THE TRANSLATOR'S PREFACE.

To many readers of this work it will doubtless be interesting to learn that in perusing the pages of *Innocencia* they will be reading the first published English translation of any work of light literature by a Brazilian author. The fact is indeed interesting, for it indicates the spread of international community of thought and ideas so characteristic of the times in which we live.

When I commenced to read *Innocencia* in the original Portuguese I had not the least idea of translating and publishing it, but, as I read on, I found my attention attracted, not only by the interest of the story, but also by the life-like picture it conveyed to me of the characters of the people and the scenery of the backwoods of Brazil. Here, thought I, in the compass of this short narrative, any reader can obtain a better idea of the rural life and scenery of inland Brazil than he could gain by studying a whole library full of books of travels in that country. Strange and almost incomprehensible and certainly strikingly original, as must appear to most English readers many of the described traits of character in the actors of the tale, they are but such as I have repeatedly witnessed in my intercourse with the Brazilian country-folk. It should however be borne in mind that the people of the described regions are such as exist from generation to generation without change of habits or ideas; but with the advent of the locomotive (which has already reached Uberaba) it necessarily brings in its train humanising influences, that will, and really do, shatter many of the old world prejudices and customs yet so rampant in the far interior of Brazil.

Wishing to obtain a confirmation, or otherwise, of my opinions of the work before submitting it to the public, I requested my friend Mr. H. W. Bates, the Secretary of the Royal Geographical Society, and the author of the well-known *Naturalist on the Amazons*, to give me the frank result of his perusal of the MS. With his kind permission I am allowed to quote his reply:

> "I have finished reading your translation of the short Brazilian novel *Innocencia*, and have been strongly interested by it. It so happens that I have had quite a course of novel-reading this winter—English, French, and American—and was getting rather *blasé*, but there is a novelty and charm in the scenes and characters of *Innocencia* which woke me up again. The plot is very simple, but not simpler than that of the famous *Paul et Virginie*, and there is great pathos in the story—not artificially worked up, but coming out quite naturally. The groundwork of the tale is its graphic picture of scenery, life, and character in rural Brazil, and the characters are drawn with wonderful truth and simple force."

From so eminent an authority on Brazil such a satisfactory corroboration of my ideas was most gratifying, and I hesitated no longer in submitting to the public a work which, whether the story it contains interests them or otherwise, will at least add considerably to any reader's knowledge of the little-known rural life and scenery of Brazil.

The author, who writes under the *nom de plume* of Sylvio Dinarte, is a distinguished Senator of the Brazilian Empire, and is one of the ablest and most popular writers in the country. He willingly and unconditionally accorded me permission to publish my translation of his work, and expressed his satisfaction by observing, "I am indeed delighted to see that my book is deemed worthy of the honour of a translation."

As to the translation, I have endeavoured to make it approach the nearest equivalent in idiomatic English, but as the author is wonderfully rich in local *patois* and proverbs, which would be comparatively unintelligible if put into actual corresponding English, I have had to take liberties in my treatment of the matter. Imagine a Frenchman putting "Barkis is willin'" or some of Sir Walter Scott's broad Scotch into French! The foreign reader must necessarily lose much of the local colouring, but here and there I have adopted the original, purposely with the intention of preserving, as much as possible, the same local colour. For instance, *Mon Dieu!* in French, or *Meu Deus!* in Portuguese, which is practically similar, receives a vastly different value to My God! in English.

JAMES W. WELLS.

Olinda, Beckenham, Kent.

CHAPTER I: THE SERTÃO[1] AND THE SERTANEJO.

The road from the town of Sant'Anna do Paranahyba[2] to the abandoned pass of Camapuan,[3] crosses a little-known and thinly-inhabited zone of the south-east part of the vast province of Mato Grosso. From that town—which is situated nearly at the junction of the territories of S. Paulo, Minas Geraes, Goyaz, and Mato Grosso—to the River Sucuriu, distant some hundred and sixty miles, one travels conveniently from habitation to habitation more or less distant one from the other. After crossinsg the river the houses become more and more rare. Long- hours are spent on the journey—even entire days—without seeing either house or inhabitant, until is reached the ranch of José Pereira, the advanced guard of those solitudes. A sound and hospitable man is he, and one who welcomes the traveller in this far-extending desert with a hearty welcome, and provides him with provisions for a journey to the distant *campos*[4] of Miranda and Piquiry, or of Vaccaria and Nioac, on the Lower Paraguay.

---

[1] The term Sertão (pronounced Sair-toung) expresses any very thinly-peopled prairie region in the distant interior of Brazil, and the inhabitants, Sertanejos (pronounced Sair-tahn-ái-jous), invariably follow the occupation of cattle breeding.

[2] In a straight line this old town is about five hundred miles in a W.N.W. direction from Rio de Janeiro.

[3] The pass, or rather portage, of Camapuan is situated in the watershed of the Parana, and Paraguay rivers, and where, in former times, the Portuguese traders gained access to the inland regions of Mato Grosso by dragging their canoes from the head waters of the tributary stream of one great river to those of the other. This overland route from the coast is now abandoned, the ascent of the Paraguay by steamer from the Plate being much preferable. [Notes, Trans.]

[4] Campos or Prairies.

Beyond this house commences the complete solitude known as the Sertão Bruto.[5] There, as one camping ground for the night succeeds the other, neither inhabited nor ruined house or thatched hut offers to the traveller a shelter from the chills of night, against the storm that threatens, or from the falling rain. Everywhere reigns the calm and peace of untilled regions. Everywhere the vegetation is virgin, as virgin as when for the first time it there burst into life.

The road that crosses these wild regions is a trail of coarse white sand, the predominating element of the soil, which is, however, fertilised by innumerable limpid gurgling brooks, whose waters are so many tributaries of the Parana or the Paraguay.

This sand, loose and coarse-grained, is bleached so white that it reflects with intensity the rays of the sun as they strike the plain. In some places it is so soft and loose that the hoofs of animals of travelling troops sink in it to their fetlocks, and many a horse or mule falls exhausted with the fatigue of a journey in such terribly heavy ground. But, from one side or other of the road, frequent paths lead the wayfarer to a firmer soil in the less beaten tracks of the cerrado[6] or jungle.

If the aspect of the road appears ever the same, its monotony is compensated for by the great variety of the landscape.

Now it is a perspective of the cerrados, not the dwarfed vegetation of the cerrados of S. Paulo and Minas, but of lusty and elevated trees, which, if they do not develop to the

---

[5]The Wild Sertão or Wilderness.

[6]Cerrados are usually a species of dwarf forests, composed of shrubs and trees of three to fifteen feet in height, more or less close to one another. Sometimes these trees attain a greater development and form the transition to capoeiras. (A good idea of the cerrados may be formed by picturing an ordinary English orchard with all the intervening spaces filled with grass and shrubs.—Note, Trans.)

CHAPTER I: THE SERTÃO AND THE SERTANEJO.

magnitude they are capable of when watered by limpid streams, still they shadow their localities with their abundant boughs, and show in their smooth bark all the strength of their alimentary sap. Now the eye gazes towards the blue horizon, far away towards vast rolling campos covered with matted, tall, yellow grass, the uninterrupted growth of ages; or else with a delicate sward brilliantly green and dotted with wild flowers. Sometimes appears a succession of luxuriant clumps of woodland, so regular and symmetrical in their disposition that their beauty equally surprises and delights the eyes of the traveller. Finally, there are barren, marshy, or dry sandy tracks, where in the hollows are thorny thickets of the lofty bority palm and the wild pine-apple.

These campos, which appear so varied in the diversity of their colours—the tall yellow grass, dry and parched, or the verdant carpet of light green—are transformations caused by the hand of some passing muleteer, who, by accident or for diversion, drops a light upon the grass already dried by the heat of the tropical sun.

The incendiary carelessly watches the effect of his work.

A breeze comes. A tongue of fire rises tremulously, as if hesitating where to precipitate itself over the vast space it contemplates. The breeze blows stronger. Instantly, from a thousand points, burst forth the chequered flames, leaping one to the other over intervening areas with the contortions of snakes writhing, darting, and gliding. Anon, a broad sheet of fire, or myriads of fiery darts, send heavenwards dense clouds of black smoke, and, rushing onwards with fierce sullen roar and startling reports, sweep over the plain, to halt only by the margin of some stream which stops the way, unless the wind, with vivacious breath carries yet onwards the work of destruction.

But when, for want of feeding, that fierce impetus is calmed, everything becomes covered with ashes. The fire, here and there detained to consume more slowly some obstacle, gradually dies away until all is extinguished, leaving as a sign of its passage the white sheet that followed its swift career.

Through the now smoke-laden atmosphere the sun peers pale and wan. The destruction is complete. The heat intense. In the air float particles of burnt grass, straw, and grains of charcoal which, in the eddies of the air, form into little vortices, and rise or fall and embrace us in a cloud of cinders, or capriciously whirling to and fro, in columns like water-spouts, seem to charge one against the other.

Melancholy reigns supreme; on every side is a gloomy, sombre perspective.

If, however, some days hence, there falls a copious rain, it would seem as if a magic wand had been passed over those sombre lands and traced such enchanted gardens as never were seen. Vegetation develops with marvellous activity. Life is transformed. There is not a spot in which the grass is not piercing the ground—the young sprouts seeming to watch, with a peeping eye, the moment to expand into liberty.

Nothing can impede that resurrection.

To hide from view the erstwhile sad scene, one night only is sufficient to spread over all a lovely carpet of bright light green, a carpet of green satin. Afterwards, gathering their strength, the flowers of the campos spring forth, and spread to the breeze of the desert their delicate petals loaded with the first offerings of their sweet perfumes.

If, however, these life-bestowing showers fail to appear, then for many months these fire-devastated campos will remain a

CHAPTER I: THE SERTÃO AND THE SERTANEJO.

cemetery of vegetation lugubriously illumined by the sun, without a shade, without a charm, without a hope of life, with all their gay flowers and verdant grasses hidden, as if sullen or sad that they have been denied the means to deck the earth with their gay colours as of yore.

In these melancholy regions not even is heard the cry of the coy perdiz[7] (a bird which is so abundant before the campos are burned), only now and then echoes over the silent wastes the prolonged cat-like scream of some hawk as it flies by overhead, or approaches the earth to seize some reptile, half scorched by the prairie fire.

The eagle-like cry of the cara-cara[8] also occasionally breaks the otherwise profound silence as, in long leaping bounds, it procures its food of insects and small snakes, or, flying close to the ground, follows a flight of turkey buzzards, directed by their keen olfactory nerves to some putrid carcase.

The cara-cara is the messmate of those foul birds. When it is hungry it will feed on carrion, and, interrupted as it may be with some sharp pecks from its amiable companions, it tears away at the unclean feast.

If the cara-cara passes within sight of a hawk, then the latter will precipitate itself upon the former with a fierce charge, and, striking it with the points of its wings, stun its antagonist, apparently only for the sake of showing its (the hawk's) incontestable superiority.

Such are the campos when unwatered by the rain. With what pleasure therefore will the Sertanejo hurry towards the capões (clumps of forest) which he sees far away, near the foothills of

---

[7] A partridge.

[8] A large carrion-hawk.

distant serras, and surrounding some spring bordered by graceful pindahybas and boritys! With what pleasure he will salute those groves of beautiful palms, the indicators of crystal water to quench his thirst and bathe his sunburnt brow!

Sometimes these palms form avenues of singular regularity in their height and disposition; but more commonly they form compact groups of noble columns, amongst which smaller and younger growths fill the intervening spaces or follow the winding courses of tributary springs.

The capões[9] at once attract attention. In the distance they appear as black spots, nearer as domes of verdure; finally, on approaching them, as islands of luxuriant foliage, each one a restful oasis for the weary limbs of the traveller exhausted with fatigue, a shade for his sun-dazzled eyes and sun-scorched face.

He hurriedly unpacks his animals and drives them to pasture where they will, and eagerly he seeks the shady recesses of the wood, where a peaceful rest and refreshing sleep restores to him new life and vigour to continue his journey. These blissful moments are, to the man of the Sertão, really incomparable and superior to everything that his imagination can idealise. Having satisfied the thirst which has parched his throat, and hastily swallowed a few spoonfuls of farinha of manioc, or of pounded maize sweetened with some pieces of rapadura,[10] he suspends his hammock, and, with a profound sigh of relief, he reposes therein his weary limbs, and negligently contemplates the pale azure sky flecked with fleeting snowy clouds, the gleaming foliage of the pale white-stemmed pindahybas, the tops of the flowering ipês, or the fronds of bority palms

---

[9]The word is Guarany Indian, and signifies "islands of forest in a sea of grass."—[Trans.]

[10]Compressed bricks of coarse sugar.

CHAPTER I: THE SERTÃO AND THE SERTANEJO.

lisping sweet music without end in the passing breeze.

How beautiful are those palms!

The smooth trunk—a stately column, light grey in colour, without a single discoloration of lichen or weather—carries at its summit a dense array of far-reaching smooth and channelled stems, which terminate in fan-like flexible leaves tremulously fluttering- in the slightest puff of air and scintillating in the rays of the sun with gleams of emerald and gold. At the springing of the leaf-stems, and well protected by solid and strong spathes, hang great bunches of golden-brown cones, so hard that, for a time, they defy even the iron beaks of the macaws. Yet what vigour these noisy screamers will employ to obtain those succulent fruits. They congregate in groups, some all crimson as a flame of fire, others of variegated colours, others, on the contrary, of deep azure blue. Holding on to leaf -stems and gravely balancing or swaying their bodies to and fro, their never-ending harsh screams resound far and wide over the immense areas of the campos, a noisy clamour without an object, unless when it is redoubled as a group dispute for the possession of the same fruit. But nearly always they are found in pairs, billing and cooing side by side.

The Sertanejo sees all this only with eyes heavy with slumber. The eyelids close drowsily, although well he knows that these groves are the haunt of the jaguar and the anaconda. He is a fatalist and confides in his destiny, and, without further effort or thought, sleeps with tranquillity.

The hours pass away. The sun glides slowly to its bed. The breeze freshens until the wind blows strong and brisk. The boritys no longer lisp their music, they wail and groan as the streaming leaves are convulsively agitated.

It is the evening that has arrived.

Then the traveller awakens; he rubs his eyes and yawns as he lazily stretches his arms, gapes, drinks a little fresh water, and then remains seated some moments gazing from one side to the other and whistling softly; finally he proceeds in quest of his horse or mule.

Once mounted he journeys on, easy in mind and body, towards a predetermined camping place for the night.

What a melancholy descends upon the earth with the fall of day!

The solitude seems to extend so far away that the aspect of its very vastness creates a sensation of timidity, by no means lessened as darkness creeps rapidly over the plains and shrouds the various scattered groups of distant shrubs and woodlands into cloud-land, for in the distance a veil of purple haze gradually unfolds itself in a soft and uniform colour, above which, here and there, the tops of lofty palms for a while longer glow in the lingering beams of departing day.

At this hour the heart throbs as with some inexplicable fear. Any sudden sounds startle one rudely; now the sad cry of the jaô in the woods, now the plaintive notes of the bucarão floating in the dewy atmosphere, or a partridge uttering its melancholy long-drawn wail, a signal for its missing mate to return to its nest ere the darkness renders that impossible.

Whosoever travels attentive to intimate impressions will tremble, in spite of himself, at heaving in these moments of sadness the toll of a churchbell far away, or maybe the strident screech of a locomotive. These sounds which create this illusion are but those of insects or of birds hidden in the bush. Yet so real and perfect is the deception, that, no matter how

CHAPTER I: THE SERTÃO AND THE SERTANEJO.

one may be convinced to the contrary, the conjured-up memories of old scenes create a craving to fly at once to those real outer worlds, to rush far away from the present sensation of uncannyness and fantasy.

The Sertanejo—who troubles not himself about anything, who hears not the harmonies of evening, who notices not the splendours of the sky, who sees not the sadness loom over the earth, who fears nothing, and lives consubstantially with the solitude—he halts, and casting a glance round about him, if in his neighbourhood he discerns some water, bad though it may be, he dismounts and unharnesses his animal, and, more for the sake of distraction than for necessity, collecting some dry wood applies to it a fire from his tinder-box.

He feels perfectly happy, for there is nothing to disturb the peace of his mind or the well-being of his body. He is not even a monologist as are other men accustomed to daily intercourse with their fellow-beings.

His thoughts are few, for he remembers only the leagues he has travelled, or computes the number he has yet to travel, in order to reach the end of his journey.

On the following day, when the dawn awakens all that virgin nature, he mechanically recommences his journey.

He observes no difference in the heavens; the clouds are the same as before; the sun passes the cardinal points; and the earth only calls for his attention when some recognised feature serves to mark a milestone on the road he travels.

"Ah!" he exclaims aloud, on seeing some gigantic tree, or a particular configuration of the land, "I have reached the big piuva tree," or, "I have arrived at the high cliff. To the camp of the Jacaré it is sixteen long miles." And glancing towards the sun he concludes, "Three hours from now I shall be lighting my fire."

There are some days when the Sertanejo will whistle. To sing is rare; even his best attempt is in a low voice, like one communing with himself rather than notes from the robust chest. His principal diversion is to reply to the cry of the partridge or to the majestic call of the timid zabelé.

To the roar of the jaguar he is indifferent; at the most he notices only the numerous tracks of the animal which intersect the road in all directions.

"What a bicho!" he murmurs, as he contemplates a footprint unusually deep in the sand. "With a good dog I would soon drive that 'diabo' into a corner and cram some lead into his muzzle."

The legitimate Sertanejo—the explorer of these deserts—is a man without family. Whilst a young man his only object of life is to see new regions, to tread the wild campos, "where the foot of man hath ne'er or rarely been," to wade through unknown rivers, explore their sources, or penetrate the depths of the virgin forest. His pride increases in proportion to the extent or importance of the journeys he has made. His greatest pleasure is to enumerate the brooks he has crossed, the streams he has named, the serras he has climbed, the swamps he has daringly traversed or, with rare patience, spent days in travelling round. Every year that ends adds something to his valuable knowledge, adds another stone to the monument of his innocent pride.

"No one can come up to me," he proudly and emphatically exclaims; "in the campos of the Vaccaria, in the sertão of the Mimoso, or in the swamps of the Pequiry, I am king."

CHAPTER I: THE SERTÃO AND THE SERTANEJO.

This presumption of royal magnificence inspires him with a mode of speech and gesticulation truly majestic in its rude manifestation. He feels assured that he can never be lost in the wilderness, and the feeling seems to carry him beyond the unknown, and allows him the license of infallibility. If he extends an arm and points over space in a certain direction, he declares peremptorily:

"In this direction, eighty miles hence, is a wild serra, and beyond it a deep river;" or, "There, twenty miles from here, is a thick, tangled forest, on the borders of a morass; if you go straight on, in five days you will come up with the camping ground of the Tatu, on the road to Cuyaba."

What he describes in one direction, with the same imperturbable serenity and assurance he will indicate in any other.

When he is describing his discoveries, the only demonstration that he will admit from any one is one of admiration. The slightest suspicion of doubt or inattention at once brings a flush of anger to his face, and his gestures speedily denote his indignation.

"You do not believe me!" he then replies. "'Then teach your own bicho[11] the road as I have told you. But listen, on the third day's journey it will be decided who is a liar and a humbug. It is one thing to converse of, but quite another to find one's way through these worlds of 'Christo.'"

When the Sertanejo begins to age, when his limbs feel tired and heavy, when the eyes become dimmed, the once sturdy arm requiring an effort to wield the hatchet that procures him

---

[11]Bicho is significative in Brazil of any mortal or immortal thing or substance, from a ghost to an elephant, a flea to a locomotive. In this case it is applied to a horse or mule.—[Transl.]

the stipe of the cabbage-palm or the succulent wild honey, it is then that he takes unto himself a wife, generally some widow or else a near relation. He builds his house and school, and eventually prepares his sons and his grandsons for the free and adventurous life which offered him so many charms in the days gone by.

These disciples, steeped in curiosity to witness the grand scenes of nature so often described, one fine day desert the paternal roof, and, scattering in various directions, each one proceeds on his solitary way—-to the confines of the Paraná, to the bushlands of S. Paulo, to the tablelands of Goyaz, or the wilderness of Mato Grosso. In fact, to anywhere, where there are desert solitudes, they go to put in practice all they have so well attended to, thinking always of the exploits of their celebrated master and progenitor.

CHAPTER II: THE TRAVELLER.

The 15tlh July, 1860, as is usually the case in winter in the interior of Brazil, was a day clear, serene, and fresh.

The sun, already high on its course, and with rays not very warm for intertropical regions, shone brightly upon the road whose aspect we have endeavoured to depict as the one leading from the town of Sant'Anna do Paranahyba to Camapuan.

At this hour, and following that road, a traveller was seen mounted on a strongly-built, pacing, flea-bitten brown mule. His physiognomy and mode of costume denoted a man of ordinary and common-place life, such as some fazendeiro or farmer of the neighbourhood returning to his home. His visible raiment comprised a broad-brimmed Chili hat encircled with a black ribbon, and a poncho of varied colours which readied to his strong, well-made riding-boots of yellow leather.

At the most he appeared to be only five-and-twenty, with a pleasing presence and an air of intelligence and decision. His features were fairly regular; eyes clear, open, and black; and beard and hair dark and closely trimmed.

In his hand he grasped a long switch, lately cut from the roadside, and which he distractedly waved in the air or with it swept aside the boughs which overhung the road.

He travelled alone, and on the occasion on which we commence this story he was passing along that beautiful piece of the road which lies between the house of Albina Lata and that of Leal, and is twenty-eight good miles beyond the fever-stricken and decadent town of Sant'Anna do Paranahyba.

This portion of the road, shaded by the trees of the sightly cerrado, although very sandy is firm, and resembles a path in a well-kept garden rather than the track of mules and waggons.

The charm of the verdant shades is here further augmented by the presence of innumerable brown and grey doves, whose incessant flutter of wings produces a sound pleasing as it is singular.

Our traveller, although he seemed distracted in attention and half immersed in his thoughts, did not appear withal to be of a morose nature or unobservant. On the contrary, for at times he would suddenly awaken from an apparent torpor and commence to sing aloud, to whistle, or else to apply spurs to his valiant beast, which promptly increased its paces, its long ears waving and beating time to its steps.

In one of those reactions against some preoccupation, he observed aloud, as he pulled out a silver watch attached to a chain of the same metal:

"Two hours hence I intend to take a siesta under the roof of Leal. It wants little to mid-day, and there is no need to hurry."

He accordingly moderated the pace of the mule, and gaping furiously with ennui, amused himself by absently switching at the passing bushes.

A short time only he thus proceeded on his way alone, for soon afterwards another traveller joined him, one mounted on an ugly and knock-kneed but very strong little horse, bathed in sweat from a fast gallop.

The new arrival, a man already advanced in years, was stout in figure, and with a face full, round, rubicund, and jovial in expression. He wore the leather hat, the striped cotton

CHAPTER II: THE TRAVELLER.

garments, and wide riding-boots of a native of Minas, and appeared—as he eventually proved—to be an inhabitant of the neighbourliood.

"Hallo there, fellow-countryman!" he exclaimed, as he moderated the pace of his animal to that of the person he interrogated; "hallo! are you going to Camapuan?"

The other looked somewhat suspiciously at the stranger who addressed him so peremptorily, and he replied evasively:

"Perhaps yes, perhaps no. But who is it who inquires my purpose?"

"Ah, excuse me," replied the former laughingly, "I did not even greet you—I am such a heedless fellow—God be with you!—There, this always happens to me. My tongue sometimes gets so crazy that it clatters in my jaws—that is, God help us, and—however, I need not tell you: water runs and so does my tongue. Look you, many times I have got into trouble—but what would you? It is an old bad habit. Not that I am a ruffianly fellow, you know. Heaven defend me from being such! I repel the idea. But a tinkling, heedless fellow—yes, a very rattletrap. As soon as I sighted you I just itched all over to talk."

The volubility with which these words were uttered somewhat startled the young man, who now scrutinised his companion with more attention, but with less reserve in his manner. Then, as he noted the merry physiognomy and good-tempered look of the talkative stranger, he could not repress a sympathetic smile as he laughingly observed:

"By what I see, the Senhor evidently loves a chat."

"Oh! don't I," replied the other. "Why, in these sertões I only feel the want of one thing; and that is the difficulty of meeting a Christian with whom I can have a bit of gossip. Ah! yes, indeed, one gets crazy here. Every one you meet has nothing to say for himself—truly, a great misfortune! I am not one of these people here, I am a Mineiro; I was born in Parahybuna, and I knew in my time people who *could* talk, and I was brought up in Mata do Rio as a human being and not as a bicho of the woods."

"Ah! The Senhor is from Minas?"

"Geraes, if you please. I was baptised at Vassouras it is true, but I am a Mineiro to the core. I knocked about all over the country before I settled in this region. That is already long ago, for I am now getting old. It is more than forty years since I left my parents."

Interrupting himself a moment he inquired, "Is the Senhor from Minas also?"

"Nhôr-não,"[12] replied the other. "I am a native of S. Paulo; I was born in the town of Casa Branca, but I was educated at Ouro Preto."

"Ah! In the imperial city?"

"Precisely."

"Then you are nearly from my old home," replied the Mineiro, laughing boisterously. "Now, who would have thought it? Yet I hastened my march when I saw your fresh tracks in the sand. There goes, I said to myself, some chap who is not in a hurry; and whipping up my little 'Penknife' I tried to catch you up so that I might not make the journey talking only to my buttons. Do you think I did any harm?"

"Não, Senhor," the young man protested with affability, "I am

---

[12]This is a corruption of *não, Senhor*—no, sir—and is an idiom peculiar to the interior provinces of Brazil.—[Trans.]

CHAPTER II: THE TRAVELLER.

much obliged to you for your attention. In this way we shall without fatigue reach the house of Leal, where I intend to repose my bones for the night."

"Oh!" exclaimed the other frankly, "our road is the same. Look you, my rich Senhor, I live two miles away from Leal, turning off to the left, and if you are not engaged to the man, do me the favour to put up under the roof of one who, if poor, is a friend to serve you. My quarters are somewhat retired from the road, but he who goes mounted like the Senhor thinks nothing of a bit of a league more of his journey."

An invitation so spontaneous and friendly could not be otherwise than appreciated, especially in those regions, and soon produced between the two travellers the familiarity that one so quickly establishes when *en route*.

"With much pleasure I will accompany you home," replied the young man. "I have never seen Leal, and, moreover, this is the first time that I have travelled in this Sertão, where it seems one has to go from resting-place to resting-place begging only for a corner in a barn or ranch to pass the night with one's attendants."

"Then bring you a troop?"

"No, only two cargo animals which carry my baggage, and a spare mule."

"Ho! ho! my friend travels like a nobleman," the Mineiro leisurely observed.

"Bah! Privations enough I have already experienced."

"Well, certainly you won't experience them in our shanty as long as you care to remain there. You won't find luxuries, it is true, nor any belongings of wealth, only such as at the best, you can obtain in these 'worlds' (regions), as four walls of upright sticks but poorly plastered over, a trestle canvas bed, good beans in abundance, some chopped herbs, rice, good roasted maize, coffee, and even possibly a loin of fresh pork."

"Now look you!" exclaimed the young man, laughing heartily. "I shall fare as well as a quartermaster-general. I want not so much, enough for me——"

"What I wish above all," interrupted his companion, "is that you will just speak straight out. If you like not your stay, say so frankly, and go away at once. In my ranch I can but put up a few people, and, as it is situated some distance away from the main road, you may perhaps want for something; in any case I will do the best I can."

After a short pause he continued:

"But I think it is already time, now that we are as two friends from the occasion of our meeting, to know with whom we are treating. I, so far as I am concerned, am called Martinho dos Santos Pereira, and my history I can tell in two 'wisps of straw.' Your title, what is it?"

"Cyrino Ferreira de Campos," replied the other traveller, "a servant to serve you."

"Thank you," replied Pereira, courteously bowing and raising his hand to his hat. "As I have just observed, my history is soon told. My people are not of an ignoble race; on the contrary, my father—whom God gave to glory—possessed some property and left to his many children an honourable and respected name. Each one of us—we were seven brothers —went his own way. I married very young and went to live in Diamantina, where I opened a store. After my wife died, I removed, first to Pinmhy, and later on to Uberaba. I then

CHAPTER II: THE TRAVELLER.

began to be disheartened with life, and calculated that as I was so far away in the backwoods I might just as well be in the Sertão. I therefore sold my hardware business and buried myself here with three slaves. I have lived twelve years in this hole, and really, and on my word of honour, I have not repented doing so. In my little fazenda there is abundance, and 'praise and glory' I have never wanted for necessaries. Not for this can I complain. Deus, Nosso Senhor Jesus Christo, has watched over me, and I consider myself well protected, especially when I think of the great misery there is in other regions. Cruz! It is not even good to talk about. Tell me one thing, however, where are you bound for?"

"Really, Senhor Pereira, I have no certain destination."

"Truly? Then are you aimlessly wandering about?"

"I will place everything before you 'on clean plates.'[13] I am travelling about these distant regions curing agues and severe fevers."

"All!" exclaimed Pereira, with manifest satisfaction, "then you are a doctor, eh? Physicians as we used to call them in bygone times."

"It is the truth," confirmed Cyrino, with, some vanity.

"Look you now! Best of all, the sop bas fallen in the honey!"

"How?"

"You will soon know. But tell me. Where did you read in the books and learn your charms and witchcraft? In the Court of the Empire?"

"No," replied Cyrino, "I studied at first in the college of Caraça; afterwards I went to Ouro Preto, where I obtained my

---

[13] An idiom expressive of "I will be thoroughly frank with you."

diploma of pharmaceutist. And," he added with some complacency, "since then I have wandered all over the west of Minas and made cures that are marvellous."

"Ah! Knowledge is a good thing—I also have a smattering of something more than mere reading and writing, although I only do that so so; but whoever is born to be a carrier, just turns, messes about, lets go, takes up, but ever ends close to the waggon. Withal then, you understand how to cure?"

"I do," affirmed Cyrino, without the least hesitation.

"Well, you tumbled most happily into my hands, Sim Senhor. A child of mine is ill with the chills—my daughter—for whose sake I have been to Sant'Anna to fetch some quinine; but there they had none of the cursed stuff, and I was returning very sad, now——"

"I bring," interrupted the other, "an abundance of remedies in my trunks. For fever and ague I have an infallible composition."

"Yes, I know; something with quinine in it. It is a holy medicine, I gave to the little one some I made from the quina of the campos, but that had but little force and no effect, so little indeed that she still has the ague."

"How many days is it since she had the last attack of cold rigors?" inquired the so-called doctor.

"To-day is the tenth day. Until now she was a lusty girl, healthy and rosy as a jambo. I can't imagine how she caught the chills. No one can rely upon that town of Sant'Anna; it is a nest of fevers. Much against my will I took her there, but she bothered me so, and as it was to see her godmother—a very good woman and of much importance, the wife of Major Mello Taques—I consented. Do you know him?"

CHAPTER II: THE TRAVELLER.

"Certainly I do."

"And are you intimate with the Major?" asked Pereira, with the view of opening a new field of chatter.

"I stayed with him when I was in the town."

"And don't you like him? Is not he just what you may call an upright man. Why, he is the chief prop of all the work in Sant'Anna: he is the tatu[14] of the place. When he wants to get up a good old gossip according to his taste he sends out to fetch the padre, and then these two soon arrange a conversation that just gives even me a surfeit. And you know he is a man of letters and much learning; he writes to the government; he is a justice of the peace and a full major, serves as the municipal judge, and is worthy of much esteem. He lives in a storied house and has a store of all sorts of goods, and the things are cheap considering the distance. And, ah! what stories can't he tell! Eh! He never finishes. The man seems to know the whole of the Empire; the vicar is nowhere. Look you, Senhor Cyrino, I will tell you something which perhaps you will think extraordinary. Sometimes I skip up to the town just to say a word or two with the Major, because with the people about here, why bless you, you can do nothing; it is tempting Providence it is. Then, as I was telling you, I galloped up to there, and got into such a conversation that it just filled me up to the brim. There is not— —"

"Excuse me interrupting you a moment," interrupted Cyrino; "but tell me, Senhor Pereira, can I do any business about here?"

"Man! It depends. Sick people there are in abundance; but they are also as mean as only they know how to be. Some distance from my house there is Coelho, who is dying, and

---
[14]The person of the most consideration.

has been dying these many years, and he is a man with plenty of coin. If you cure him, perhaps you will come in for some of his coppers. All the rest is more or less a rude mob of people. By-the-by, have you plenty of the quinine of commerce?"

"I have," responded Cyrino, "but it is dear.'"

"That it is dear, I know well. But that you have it, is enough, because here in these regions ague is everywhere."

Senhor Pereira then commenced to enumerate the ills that had attacked him during his life; a few only, it is true, but they were serious, and with this theme at his disposal he found sufficient to talk about until he was nearly exhausted for want of breath.

His companion was silent, and listened with the inattention of one preoccupied with thought, or, in any case, quite heedlessly to all that his new friend related, awakening only from his apathy to instigate with his voice, or to spur on, the movements of his mule whenever that animal seemed inclined to pause for a rest or to seize a mouthful of some wayside grass.

Pereira at last noticed the inattention of his companion.

"You are in a sad kind of mood," said he. "Have you left any of your belongings behind you?"

"Man, to be frank with you," replied Cyrino, giving vent to a sigh, "I have left something, and this something is a debt, a debt of honour—cards."

"That is bad," replied the Mineiro seriously. "That 'demonio' and women are the cause why so many crosses grow by the roadside. But is it a big sum?"

"Three hundred milreis" (£30 about).

CHAPTER II: THE TRAVELLER.

"That is a lump, truly. Who did you play with?"

"With Totó Siqueira of Sant'Anna. He wanted to stop my departure, but I promised to send him the amount from Sucuriu by my servant. I gave him a note to that effect, and just now I am thinking how I shall obtain the money even when I get there."

"If those who owe you pay you, you are all right. In any case put the screw on to the sick ones a little."

"You cannot imagine," replied Cyrino, with true feeling, "how miserable this wretched debt has made me. It is not for the sake of the money—that does not trouble me—but it is because I have been gambling, a thing I never did before in all my life, and that is the truth."

"Therefore, meu Senhor," proceeded Pereira, "let this serve as a lesson; and take a word of caution: beware of these people of the Sertão, not exactly of those who live in decent homes, you know, but rather of casual strangers, muleteers, carriers, and such like, for they are more often than not only gangs of gamblers, armed with marked cards and all kinds of shuffling tricks, and for a mere straw they will stick a knife into the stomach of a Christian, or let fly the contents of a pistol at the head of a companion as if it were only a rotten melon. Besides, when the demon of play seizes hold of one, he takes up his abode in him, and straightway shuts out all feeling of shame. For the attraction of women there is perhaps some excuse, but once you are enticed into play and lotteries, the sooner you move on the better. I once had an uncle who lived in Corredor, about eight miles this side of Camapuan, and who worked on his lands the whole year round just to go to Sucuriu and play until he lost his last copper."

Pereira, in possession of so wide a subject, related stories innumerable, some were lugubrious in their incidents, others jocular, some were true, and others were invented for the occasion.

Meanwhile, as the two men had now covered several miles of their journey, the sun had already approached the horizon, and from the west arrived the first wafts of the evening breeze.

"We," observed the Mineiro, "with our conversation, have allowed the animals to crawl along. But we are already at my road. Here it is, Senhor Cyrino; that one ahead leads on to Leal; my fazenda lands commence at this point, and, skirting the road, extend thence to far away in the distance.

On saying these words he left the main road on his right and followed a wide open- road, which, with many turns and windings, led towards a limpid stream. The animals, hearing the murmur of running water, at once quickened their paces, and soon afterwards, on reaching the brook, they plunged in breast high, quenching their thirst as they advanced step by step against the current in search of the clearest water.

"Don't let your beast overload himself," observed Pereira. "Up-la!" he continued, as he pulled the reins of his horse and gave him a friendly pat on its extended neck. "Up-la! my Penknife! Let us rather go and fill up the emptiness with good corn."

On the further side of the stream, a narrow path led through some woods thick with undergrowth, and then afterwards joined a broad road, where the travellers put their animals to a half gallop.

Finally, with the sun already low, there appeared in sight, above the outline of the darkening trees of a thick wood, the

CHAPTER II: THE TRAVELLER.

peak of a mast of S. John, which the Mineiro saluted merrily as the neighbourhood of his cherished home.

Before, however, we penetrate therein, let us say who was that youth who thus travelled with the pompous title of doctor, and, what is more, was armed with authority to go where he pleased to apply remedies and assure miraculous cures.

CHAPTER III: THE DOCTOR.

Cyrino de Campos was born, as he had told Pereira, in the province of S. Paulo, in the peaceful and pretty town of Casa Branca, about two hundred miles from the coast. Son of a vendor of drugs (who called himself chemist, and added to his trade the functions of a post-office master), Cyrino grew up under the parental eyes until he reached the age of twelve years, when he was sent at one festival time, and with many kindly recommendations, to an old uncle and godfather, an inhabitant of Ouro Preto, Minas Geraes.

This relation—a bachelor, and by disposition extremely morose, misanthropical, and given to the practice of the most penurious habits—received the boy surlily and with manifest discontent; for the presence of a stranger would naturally interrupt the manner of complete retirement to which he had been addicted for so many years.

He was an old man who yet retained the fashions of his youth in wearing knee-breeches and buckle shoes, powdered hair and a pig-tail.

He was reputed to be wealthy, so much so, that throughout the city of Ouro Preto it was affirmed that he was a thorough miser, the public voice declaring that his gold, and that no small sum, was buried in holes he had made in the floor of his bedroom.

"My little friend," observed his godfather to Cyrino a few days after his arrival, "you may rest assured that, for the merest trifle, I will drive every grain of dust out of your jacket with a good cudgelling', so just be advised in time, and take care to conduct yourself as straight as a spindle."

CHAPTER III: THE DOCTOR.

The boy, terrified, retired to a dark corner of the house, where, all the long evening until slumber relieved his feelings, he passed the dreary hours in bitter tears and in regretful memories of the happy days passed with his old playfellows on the luxuriant grass lands of the outskirts of Casa Branca, and, above all, in yearning longings for the loving kindness of his mother.

After having relieved himself of such a precautionary admonition, the uncle then proceeded to the house of certain padres who possessed some influence in the neighbouring college of Caraça, and with them he made arrangements for the admission of his nephew into that establishment for clerical instruction.

With his natural cunning, he succeeded without much difficulty in obtaining his desires, and in paying the costs with compound interest merely by the aid of tempting promises.

"At present," he observed, or rather he hinted to the padres, "I can do nothing for the education of the lad, but—in short—I am already an old man, you know, and—and some day I—I will try to prove that I do not forget the good padres who have helped me so much."

The priests unhesitatingly construed his vague promises into an intended legacy of a good round sum, and, relying upon such an eventuality, it was decided that Cyrino should be admitted to the college.

The knowledge of the want of natural protection generally causes boys to become docile and resigned to their fate. The country lad therefore preserved a timid silence as he passed the threshold of the home, where, withal, he would but sadly pass the best days of his youth in masticating Latin, stammering Telemachus, and, day and night, intoning in a falsetto voice the service of the Church.

Unquestionably the old uncle had done a very good stroke of business to attain his object with the expenditure only of words which cost him nothing; moreover, he clung to life so tenaciously, that, eventually, he had the satisfaction of seeing carried to their last home in the cemetery two of the padres in whom he had created such hopes of inheriting some of his wealth.

Finally, as he also had to pay the universal tribute, one fine day he died when least expected, but uttering strict injunctions to attend to his will, which was promptly examined with an eagerness worthy of a better cause.

A last will and testament it was, it is true; yet it was not merely a testament only, but an extensive legal argument, and all done in the handwriting of the old man; but of bars of gold or of piles of notes, not the shadow of a vestige nor a word of mention.

The house was searched from top to bottom; the floors were taken up; the walls were sounded; the furniture was broken; yet all in vain, nothing appeared, nothing indicated the hiding place of the riches nor gave any clue to guess their whereabouts.

Then it was discovered that the old fraud—once a follower of the arch-rebel Xavier, or Tiradentes (the Tooth Drawer)—was really what he had always professed to be, a man without a penny, and who had philosophically lived at the cost of his neighbours on the credit of the wealth with which, they in their imaginations had endowed him.

His last testament was one long satire, half jocular, half ironical, like a mocking laugh from the tomb, and endorsed by

CHAPTER III: THE DOCTOR.

the sarcastic legacy of his library, which, in a pompously-worded codicil, he left to the padres of Caraça, "with the end," said he, "to aid the education of youths and further the good intentions of their honoured and virtuous directors."

On searching for the books, an old trunk was discovered filled with the remains of volumes destroyed by white ants. Amid cries of indignation and horror, these were, by order of the padres, immediately committed to the flames of an *auto da fe*; for the fragments of the books showed them to be translations in Portuguese of *The Ruins* of Volney, *The Man of Nature*, *The Philosophical Dictionary* of Voltaire, *The Quotations* of Pigault-Lebrun, *The War of the Gods* of Parny, and the romances of the Marquis of Sade.

The consequences of this posthumous joke, which destroyed to the root the conceit of a lifetime, was the immediate exclusion of Cyrino from the college of Caraça.

He was then eighteen years old, and, although an odium was attached to him on account of his relationship to his singular and deceased protector, yet, being active and intelligent, he succeeded in obtaining a situation as an assistant in a small drug store, where, amongst medicines and prescriptions, he found himself returning to the old associations of his parental home.

The work was light; the preparation of prescriptions occurring so seldom that the pharmaceutical ingredients remained for entire months in their chipped and mouldy flasks waiting for some one to think of removing them from their dusty oblivion.

Amidst a small population, for a simple seller of drugs to become practically a member of the medical faculty there is but one step. In due time Cyrino began to acquire some practice in the art of prescribing, and, by constantly studying the medical work of Chernoviz, he became so familiar with its pages, that, with some medicines in his trunk, he one day set out on a voyage of discovery in the neighbouring districts in a search for patients requiring his services.

It was on these journeyings that he commenced to receive the appellation of "doctor;" and, to somewhat justify a claim to such a title, he left the service of the drug seller, and, matriculating in the School of Pharmacy of Ouro Preto, he duly received from the President of the Province the diploma of chemist and druggist.

No sooner was he in possession of this desirable document than Cyrino made a final departure, and proceeded to travel through the inhabited regions of the Sertão, to cure, bleed, cut, and slash, uniting to a limited knowledge of some value such ideas as his experience indicated or that popular opinion or superstition called for.

The whole of his knowledge was based on Chernoviz, ever his inseparable "vade-mecum," his golden book. Day and night it was in his hands; day and night he consulted its pages, by the side of his camp fire or by the bed of the sick.

Chernoviz, say the authorities, contains many errors and much irrelevant and useless matter; however, in the interior of Brazil it is a work that incontestably has done good service, and one whose teachings have the force of those of the Evangelists.

Cyrino was so familiar with every page of his copy that he could at once unhesitatingly open it at any part he required, and by its means he obtained a fund of instruction that was correct up to a certain point, and with which was happily united the natural study of the useful and littleutilised herbs

CHAPTER III: THE DOCTOR.

of the campos and forest.

With the object of increasing his resources in indigenous medicinal herbs, he at times extended his tours beyond the inhabited regions, and only returned to his town when in want of such drugs as he could not obtain from Nature.

Finally, being naturally disposed to the complete freedom of action of the life of a wanderer, he resolved on undertaking a journey to Camapuan and the south of Mato Grosso; not only with the intention of extending his range of operations, but also with the view of satisfying his desires to explore new and distant lands.

The young man was naturally of a generous disposition, and his mind was incapable of breeding unworthy thoughts; nevertheless, in the depths of his character there had already taken root certain habits of pride or a somewhat excessive self-esteem, the natural balance to a more or less share of acquired quackery, arising not only from his insufficient knowledge, but more especially from the narrow world of thought in which he had always lived.

In any case, with all his defects, he was far superior to the ordinary peripatetic quack of the Sertão, such as one so often meets in those regions, and who is usually a man of the most crass ignorance, but surrounded by prerogatives of the most exceptional character. He enters everywhere; he penetrates the utmost seclusion of home life; he occupies the best seat at the guests' table, the softest bed in the house. In short, the doctor is a sacred person fallen from heaven, and, for many miles round, he attracts not only the sick, the halt, and the blind, but also fanatical hypochondriacs, who for years having prescribed for themselves or followed the advice of neighbours, now come to tender to these Messiah doctors all their most ardent hopes for their longed-for convalescence.

CHAPTER IV: THE HOME OF THE MINEIRO.

When the travellers reached the entrance to the yard containing the farm buildings of Pereira, four or five lean and hungry dogs dashed towards them, welcoming their master with noisy yelps of joy. Some fowls scurried away at a run; two roosters, already perched for the night on the ridge of the roof of an outhouse, crowed lustily; and, from various holes and corners, big pigs and little pigs here and there peeped with their small and sleepy eyes, and wondered at the commotion.

From the interior of the habitation soon appeared a poorly-clad and aged negress, her head and shoulders enveloped in a coarse cotton cloth.

"Ho, ho, there! Ah, Maria Conga!" called Pereira, "What is there new about here?"

"A blessing, meu Senhor," the slave petitioned by extending her open hand as she somewhat slowly approached.

"God make thee holy," brusquely responded the Mineiro. "How fares the child 'Nocencia?"

"Nhia-nha[15] has got the ague."

"That I know well, but how has she fared since the day before yesterday until now?"

"Every day when the hour conies 'nha' clatters her jaws, Sim Senhor."

---

[15]Nha-nha is a negro term applied to the eldest or only daughter of a family, pronounced Een-yah een-yah.—[Transl.]

"Humph! What is bad is that the attacks have not lessened. Well, we shall see presently. And dinner? Is it ready? I am quite done up with hunger. What say you, Senhor Cyrino?" he asked, as he turned to his companion.

"I also can manage to eat something. We have reason to— —"

"Well then," interrupted Pereira, "put your foot on the ground and press hard, for the soil is ours. My house, as I have already told you, is a poor one, but it will fill you and is closed against no one."

Then, setting the example, he removed the harness from his little horse and left it to find its way to some outbuildings which served as stables.

Cyrino also dismounted, but, as he entered a species of verandah with a thatched palm-leaf roof which shaded the whole front of the house, he paused, and his gestures and physiognomy showed some vexation of mind.

"There now, Senhor Pereira," he exclaimed, beating the heel of his boot with an ear of maize, "it is only now that I remember that my baggage will follow the road to Leal, and leave me here without my clothes or my remedies. What a nuisance! We ought to have waited at the turn off of your road."

The Mineiro, with a broad grin on his homely rubicund face, exclaimed:

"Ho! ho! Is the doctor then such a greenhorn at travelling? Do you think then that I did not leave some notice for your people? Don't you remember that branch I laid in the middle of the main road, where we left it?"

"Truly I do," replied Cyrino.

"Well then. Your men will very soon be on our tracks. Let us

CHAPTER IV: THE HOME OF THE MINEIRO.

enter within, for the hunger is gripping me enough, I can tell you."

The abode of Pereira consisted of a grassthatched-roof house, capacious in area but low in height. Under a spacious verandah in front of the house, a wide doorway, bordered on each side by a narrow, unglazed, but shuttered window, gave access to a spacious front room. The front wall of the house, possibly on account of the weight of the roof, was sensibly bulged out of the perpendicular, and some longitudinal cracks therein showed that some important repairs were urgently necessary to that structure of sticks and clay.

On the right side of the house was a big thatched barn the sides of which consisted of a framework holding in place upright bamboos, from the spaces between which issued a constant supply of heads of maize, a supply largely due to the excavating operations of the pigs, who were never far away from this porcine paradise.

The roof of the verandah was thatched with burity-palm leaves and supported by thick stems of bamboos, and, extending along the whole front of the house, constituted a convenient shelter for such guests as on the occasion of some festival might exceed the ordinary accommodation of the hospitable habitation.

The interior of the house comprised two distinct divisions. The front part consisted of one large room, accessible only by the door that led into it from the outer verandah. The rest of the house formed the sanctuary of the family, and, being without any internal communication with the front room, it was completely secluded from the sight and intrusion of strangers. The earthen floor of the front room showed on it many signs of log-fires, the smoke of which had covered with a thin coating of brown polish the rafters and thatch overhead, making them resemble varnished rosewood in colour.

"This," said Pereira on entering the front room and seating himself on a three-legged stool, "belongs to my guests. A few only come this way, but anyhow it is as well to be always prepared for them. My own people live in the back part of the house."

He pointed to the blank wall facing the entrance door of the room, and made a gesture to indicate that the house extended beyond it.

"Senhor Pereira," said Cyrino, reclining himself on a solid wooden couch, "pray do not inconvenience yourself about me in any way whatever. Just imagine that no one is here."

"Well then," returned the Mineiro, "rest yourself a little, while I go inside to hear what news there is. The hour is one for eating rather than for reposing; but meanwhile lie down while you wait, for when one is tired that is a more comfortable position than sitting or standing."

The guest did not refuse the invitation. He removed his poncho, pulled off his riding-boots, and doubling them up, he utilised them for a pillow.

When one assumes a horizontal position after many miles of riding in Brazil, slumber is the inevitable and speedy sequence. Quickly, therefore, the eyelids of the young man closed in sleep, and his breast heaved with a peaceful respiration.

He had already slept for an hour and a half, and would probably have slept much longer, if he had not been awakened by the noise of the arrival of a troop of animals and the cries of men as they unloaded the cargos.

CHAPTER IV: THE HOME OF THE MINEIRO.

Senhor Pereira, with a jovial air, appeared at that instant at the doorway, saying:

"Now then, what did I not tell you, eh?"

"It is a fact; now I am perfectly contented."

"And you have had a pretty long snooze?"

"Yes, an hour perhaps."

"At least, if not more. All this time I havebeen at the bedside of 'Nocencia, who trembled with cold as if she was in Ouro Preto with the hoar frost in the streets."

"Is she no better then?"

"Not at all. When you have eaten something you shall see her. She is so altered that she looks as if she had been ill for two months."

"Happily," observed Cyrino, with some petulance, "here am I to put her on her feet again."

"Heaven aid you!" cried Pereira, with a father's anxiety. "Halloa! What ho! You boys there!" he shouted to the two men who had just arrived. "You men can put up in the ranch yonder. You will find water close by, and there is no want of firewood; all you have to do is to stretch out your hands. Look you give a full ration to the mules. Make the most of the corn while you can, it is the support of the animal. I sell it cheap, two heads for a copper, and there are no poor weakly grains in them, but all sound, ripe, and big. Halloa there! Maria Conga, get on with this, put dinner on the table!"

The indications of Pereira to the men were duly attended to, and the old negress, answering to the call, proceeded to spread upon the wide, roughly-planed table, a cotton tablecloth, coarse in texture but snowy white in colour; on it she poured the contents of two gourds of coarsely-pounded maize, and then placed a soup plate of blue earthenware and a metal fork and spoon by its side.

"Sit down, doctor," said Pereira to Cyrino, "I will not help you to clean up, because I have already had something in the back room. Pardon me if the food is not to your liking."

At this moment Maria Conga returned with two smoking dishes, one filled with black beans and the other with rice.

"And the green vegetables?" inquired Pereira. "Are there none?"

"Nhor-sim" (Sim Senhor), "I will bring them directly," replied the negress, and promptly performing another journey, she produced the required additions to the meal.

The Mineiro again apologised for the insufficiency of quantity and rough preparation of the food.

"I do not provide you with a loin of pork to-day, but the promise will not be forgotten, of that you can rest assured."

"I am indeed contented with what there is,'" protested Cyrino, and, by the vigorous way in which he attacked the repast, he evidently spoke with sincerity.

"Maria," said Pereira to the slave, who, at some distance from the table, remained standing with folded arms, "bring some of this afternoon's sugar-syrup and coffee with sugar."

The two things called for being duly produced, Cyrino completed his dinner with visible satisfaction.

"Ah!" he exclaimed, as he stretched his arms, "feel now just as compact as an egg. The beans were excellent. Praised be

CHAPTER IV: THE HOME OF THE MINEIRO.

Nosso Senhor Jesus Christo, who has given me these good quarters."

"Amen!" responded Pereira.

"Now, my friend," said the young man after a short pause, "I am at your orders. Can we see your little invalid? We may, perhaps, be able to take advantage of the opportunity of an intermission of the fever to attack it promptly. I do not like delays in these cases."

A slight cloud of gloom stole over the face of the Mineiro; he frowned somewhat, and an expression of disquietude appeared on his brows.

"Later on," he said, with some precipitation.

"Not at all," objected Cyrino. "I tell you that the sooner you attend to it the better it will be."

"Why are you in such a hurry?" inquired Pereira suspiciously.

"I?" replied Cyrino, without perceiving the intention; "I am not so in the least. It is for the good of the young woman."

The eyes of Pereira flashed with sudden brilliancy.

"And how know you that my daughter is a young woman?" he exclaimed, with vivacity.

"Well now, was it not you yourself who told me so on the road?"

"Ah! truly. She is not yet, however, a young woman. Fourteen—or fifteen years old at the very most. Say fifteen years and a half. Quite a child, you know, poor little tiling!"

"Well," replied the youth, "let it be as you like. Whenever you want me, send to fetch me. Meanwhile I will look through my trunks while I wait, and get some remedies, so as to have them ready at hand."

"Very good," acquiesced Pereira, "put your things in that corner, and you may rest assured nobody will touch them. As to my daughter—I will return directly—er—I will just take a glance inside there—and—er—er—afterwards—well, we will talk about it then."

CHAPTER V: THE PRECAUTION.

The sun had long disappeared and darkness had set in before Pereira returned to Cyrino.

"Doctor," said he, "now you can come in to see the little one. Her pulse is as soft as cotton yarn, and she has not the least fever."

"That is good," responded Cyrino; and quickly gathering in his hand the materials he had taken from his trunk, he closed the lid and arose to his feet.

Before leaving the room, Pereira, with the air of one who had to communicate something serious and at the same time of difficult confession, detained his guest. After some moments of hesitation he commenced:

"Senhor Cyrino, I am a man naturally of a very good temper, always ready to serve any one, sociable, outspoken, and frank, as you have very well seen."

"Certainly," assented the other.

"'Very well, but—er—I am very suspicious. The doctor is about to enter the interior of my home, and—I don't know, but—I must ask you to be discreet, and— —"

"Oh! Senhor Pereira!" interrupted Cyrino, without much surprise, for he was aware of the jealous care with which the men of the Sertão guard their home circles from the gaze of the profane. "I have been received in the bosoms of many families, and I know how to comport myself as I ought to."

The face of the Mineiro expanded a little.

"You see," said he, with some diffidence, "the doctor is truly no barefooted vagabond, but it is always as well to be cautious. And as there is now no other remedy, I will tell you all my secrets. With the favour of God they will shame no one, but generally I do not like my tongue to clatter about my home affairs. Listen. My daughter 'Nocencia completed eighteen years of age last Christmas, and she is a girl who by her appearance might well pass for a lady of the cities. She is shy and timid in her manner, it is true, but beautiful as she is good and virtuous. Alas! poor little thing! she was brought up motherless and here in these Sertões. I have another child, a son, a big fellow, bearded and strong—he is now working on a farm near Rio. Well, that's neither here nor there," continued Pereira, relapsing little by little into his habitual garrulity; "however, when I saw the girl assume the proportions of a woman, I at once set about getting her married— —"

"Ah! she is married?" inquired Cyrino.

"She is, and yet she is not. The thing has been talked about. Hereabouts, there is a wellto-do man who is accustomed to go with the droves of cattle to S. Paulo—perhaps the Senhor knows him?—the Manecão Doca."

"No," replied Cyrino, shaking his head.

"Well, he *is* a proper man for activity and work. There is no one like him. He rides throughout all these Sertões, and drives such herds of cattle as would astonish you. They also say that he has lots of bichos of his own, and I believe it, for he is very careful and spends little, and women have little attractions for him. On one occasion, when he was stopping here—there, just imagine, in that very identical spot where you are now standing—I spoke to him about marriage; that is, I gave him some hints, because for the welfare of their little women-folk

CHAPTER V: THE PRECAUTION.

parents ought to make this their business. Don't you think so!"

"Without doubt," Cyrino assented, "you have every reason."

"Well then, at first, Manecão was very doubtful, but when I showed him the little one—ah! then he sung another song altogether. Ah! but she *is* a girl!"

And Pereira, forgetful of his precautions, expressed his sense of supreme admiration for his daughter by placing the tips of his fingers to his coarse lips and waving a kiss to his companion.

"It is true," he continued, "she is now somewhat altered, but when she is in health she is, ah! as rosy as the mangaba of the moorlands. Her hair is long and as fine as silk, a delicate nose, and *such* killing eyes. You would not think her the daughter of one who is— —"

Paternal love carried Pereira beyond prudence to give vent to such praise, and so it seemed to suddenly occur to him, for quickly repressing himself, he observed, with manifest hesitation:

"This obligation to get the women married is just the devil! If they do not, you never know what will happen, and yet if they marry they may fall into the hands of some rascally husband. One lives in a glass bottle that any one can crack. Well, my daughter so far has honoured my name. The Manecão will be responsible for her when he has her for his own. With petticoat people you never can rely on anything. Cruz! While the devil rubs an eyelid they will utterly ruin a family."

This injurious sentiment with regard to women is common throughout the Sertão, and brings for immediate and practical consequences the rigorous seclusion in which they are maintained, the prearranged marriage of children by relatives, and, above all, the numerous crimes committed. Yet, withal, seldom is suspected the possibility of an intrigue between members of a family and a stranger.

Pereira unfolded all these ideas and strongly applauded the prudence of such preventive measures.

"I repeat," he said, with choler, "with women you never know where you are. Our forefathers of the olden time did well. Then, the young women had to walk as straight as a spindle. The slightest suspicion of a side glance, and, pah! down came the stick. Why, they say now, that up in the cities—Uumph! Detestable!—there is no girl, no matter how poor she is, who does not know how to read and scratch a pen on paper—that they are allowed to go to public parties with lowneck dresses, and that they dance, speak in loud voices, and show their teeth. to any fashionable ruffian. Cruz! That is altogether too much. Don't ill-treat the poor little things, say I, but it is not necessary to give wings to ants. When they get stalky, let a festival be arranged to marry them to some decent fellow or some cousin, and have done at once with the bother. Also," he added, as he pulled down the lower eyelid of his right eye with his forefinger, "caution, keep your eyes open, and don't be beguiled by those who come and try to please you with too, too flattering ways. My daughter——"

Pereira now completely altered his tone.

"Ah! Poor little thing! From her, no harm can come. She is a little dove from Heaven. So good, so lovable! Is she a witch? I can do nothing with her. Only when I think of handing her over to a man, the thought quite upsets me. It is, however, necessary. Years ago—I ought to have acted in this matter—but I don't know—every time I think of it my soul sinks to my

CHAPTER V: THE PRECAUTION.

feet. She is also a girl not brought up as others are. Ah! Senhor Cyrino, these children are parts of one's heart that one has to tear from his body to let wander in this world of Christo."

A tear-drop glistened in the father's eyes.

"My son is living, Heaven only knows where! If I were to die this instant, the little one would be left in complete abandonment. Yes, it is indeed necessary to finish this uncertainty. Besides, Manecão promised to leave her here at home, and in that way all will be arranged—that is, remedied —for a married daughter no longer belongs to her father."

There ensued a moment of silence.

"Now," continued Pereira, with a certain restraint, "that I have told you all, I ask you one thing. See only the invalid, and do not look for 'Nocencia, I have spoken with you thus, for it was my duty. No one man, except the closest relations of this, your servant, has placed a foot in my daughter's room— this I will swear—only in cases like this of extreme necessity —"

Cyrino here somewhat impatiently interrupted the observation of his host. "Senhor Pereira, I have already told, and again I tell you, that, as a medical man, I am accustomed to mix with families and to respect them. That is my duty, and until now, *graças a Deus*, my reputation has been, and is, good. About women, I hold not your opinions, neither do I consider them reasonable. However, it is useless for us to discuss them, as I well know that yours were long ago confirmed, and what is born crooked, only very late, perhaps never, will become straight. Do not misunderstand my words. You spoke to me with frankness, I also with frankness wish to respond. In my opinion, women are as good as us, although they are women; it is therefore not right to discredit them so much, and make so much of men. Well, these ideas of yours may serve you well, but it is an old custom of mine to contradict no one, so that I may live in peace with others, and merit the treatment from them which I have a right to expect. Let every one take care of himself; God watches over all, and no one wishes to be the ferule of the world."

This profession of faith, uttered in a superior and quasi-dogmatical tone of voice, appeared to create some degree of impression upon Pereira, who applauded it with an expressive movement of the head as though he appreciated the conceits and fluency of the phrases.

CHAPTER VI: INNOCENCIA.

After giving his explanations to Cyrino, the Mineiro experienced a greater degree of confidence in his medical adviser, and consequently was more at ease in his mind.

"Then," said he, "if you like, let us go at once and see our little invalid."

"With much pleasure," Cyrino promptly replied, and leaving the room he accompanied Pereira, who proceeded by a roundabout way towards the back door of the house, and in order to do so he had to pass through two fences that shut off the rear portion of the premises from the front. Facing the back of the house an orchard of magnificent orange- trees, all heavily laden with bloom, perfumed the atmosphere with the scent of the white and odorous blossoms.

"This place," said the Mineiro, pointing towards the orchard, "is frequented every day by great numbers of blackbirds. 'Nocencia loves to hear the music of their songs, and her favourite place to do her sewing is to sit out here under the trees. Ah! She is a girl——"

Stopping for a moment on the threshold of the door, while a beaming expression of joy gleamed over his rubicund face, he continued:

"You cannot imagine—sometimes that child will ask such questions that quite knock me over. We have a book in the house—one of the time of my defunct grandfather—well, would you believe it, if she didn't actually ask me to teach her to read! What an idea! Eh? Then again, a short time ago she told me that she wished she had been born a princess. I replied to her, 'But do you know what it is to be a princess?' 'I know,' she said, quite calmly; 'a young woman who is very good and very beautiful, who wears a crown of diamonds on her head, many jewels round her throat, and who governs all the men.' I felt quite staggered. But if you could only see the way she has with the little bichos (birds and animals), you would think that she was talking to them, and that they understood her. Any kind of animal on approaching the feet of 'Nocencia becomes as lame and docile as a newly-born calf. All, if I were to tell you all the stories about this girl I should never stop! Let us enter; that is better."

When Cyrino entered the sleeping-room of the daughter of the Mineiro, it was so dark that at his first glance about him he could only vaguely distinguish the forms of various pieces of old-fashioned furniture and a large bedstead occupying a corner of the room, and on which some person reposed.

Pereira called aloud for a light. The old negress Maria appeared with a candle, when both men approached the side of the bed of the invalid, who, hastily drawing over herself a thick coverlet of Minas cotton, turned her gaze towards the newcomers.

"Here is the doctor," said Pereira to her, "who has come to cure thee, little one."

"Good evening, Dona," saluted Cyrino.

A gentle, timid voice murmured some unintelligible reply, and the medical adviser, seating himself on a stool by the bedside, proceeded to examine the pulse of the invalid.

Despite the pallor of illness and the dim, flickering light of the candle, now placed on a bracket against the wall above her, it was easily seen that Innocencia was really dazzlingly, bewilderingly beautiful. Her face was Madonna-like in its

CHAPTER VI: INNOCENCIA.

form and sweet expression—such an one as the old masters loved to depict for their saints and Virgin Maries. It was grave and expressive, but without their sadness, and perfect in its oval outline; her brow, white, broad, and open; her eyebrows, long and pencilled, while the large, half-closed eyelids were fringed with lashes so long that they shadowed the graceful contour of her cheeks. Her nose was delicate in form and slightly aquiline, and the pearly gleams of her teeth were revealed by the partly-open lips of the beautiful little mouth. From under the sheet of cotton, which enveloped her head like a hood, a few massive locks of raven-black hair here and there strayed in luxurious abandonment. As she withdrew her arm from under the coverings, the embroidered garment in which she was clad became disarranged, and exposed to view a glimpse of a neck of alabaster whiteness.

Abundant reason therefore had Cyrino to suddenly feel his hand become cold and somewhat tremulous as he endeavoured to examine the pulse of so gentle a patient.

"Well, then?" inquired the father.

"There is not the least fever now," the youth replied, but with his eyes riveted in manifest surprise upon the face of Innocencia.

"And what is to be done?"

"To take at once a sudorific of an infusion of the leaves of the bitter orange, and see if we can establish a free transpiration; then at midnight you must call me, and I will give the Dona a dose of quinine."

The young woman raised her eyes and gazed attentively at Cyrino as she listened to the directions which should restore her to health.

"She has not the least appetite," observed the father; "for nearly three days she has lived only on liquids, and the fever is so constant that it does not look like ague."

"Never mind," replied the young man. "Tomorrow the fever will leave her, and a week hence your daughter will be on her feet for certain. It is I who guarantee it."

"Deus speaks with your tongue," cried Pereira joyously.

"Her colour will soon return," continued Cyrino.

Innocencia flushed slightly and turned her face to the pillow.

"Why do you fold this sheet about you?" the young man inquired, as he pointed to her wrapped-up head.

"For nothing," she timidly replied.

"Do you feel any headache?"

"Nhôr-não" (No, sir).

"Well, then, remove the wrapper. It is always well to keep the head cool, and also unplait your hair; let it be all loose."

Pereira carried out the directions, and soon the pale face of the invalid was framed in a sweeping mass of luxuriant hair, black as the heart of the cabiuna-tree, and so long that it would have reached to below her waist. It had been braided in plaits which twice encircled her head.

"It is also necessary," continued Cyrino, "to have the room well aired day and night, and to place the bed in a line with the east and west."

"I will have it turned to-morrow," said the Mineiro.

"Good; but to-day then, or, better still, at once, let her have the sudorific, and, for the present, close up all the doors and

CHAPTER VI: INNOCENCIA.

windows. At midnight, more or less, I will come and give the medicine. Calm your spirit. Dona, and pray two Ave-Marias in order that the quinine may have its due effect."

"Nhôr-sim" (Yes, sir), lisped the invalid.

"The light does not pain your eyes?" inquired Cyrino, approaching her to steal one more glance at her face.

"No."

"That is a good sign. I believe that the attack will soon prove to be nothing serious," and saluting his patient by saying, "Until soon, little lady," he turned to Pereira and signified his readiness to depart.

The latter beckoned to some one in a dark corner of the room. "Tico," cried he, "come here."

At the call, there came forward a curious specimen of humanity in the form of a little shrivelled-up dwarf. Although his brow was furrowed with rugged wrinkles like those of an old man, the gleam of the bright eyes and the black hair showed that his age was not very far advanced. His little legs, somewhat bowed, terminated in great broad feet, which, without any serious alteration, might easily serve for those of some web-footed bird.

This singular being was clad in a dark smock and trousers, the latter evidently having been built for an ordinary person, for the extremities had to be turned up, and so formed very voluminous rolls around his ankles. A roofless hat of palmito straw covered, or rather encircled, his head, and allowed a mass of tangled and knotted locks of hair to be seen.

"Ho! ho!" exclaimed Cyrino, on seeing this object enter within the rays of light. "Truly this is only a part of somebody."

"'Now, don't you ridicule my Antonio;" replied Pereira with a smile. "He is small, it is true, but what there is of him is good. Is not that so, my manikin?"

The little man grinned, and showed rows of white pointed teeth,[16] but the effect was more allied to a grimace than to a smile; at the same time he bestowed upon Cyrino an inquisitive and penetrating glance.

"You must know, doctor," continued Pereira, "that this creature hears perfectly everything that is said. He understands all, but cannot speak, that is, he can pronounce one or two words, but at considerable trouble, and the effort makes him nearly burst with rage. When he attempts to explain something, it is just a gabble of six hundred sounds, and amidst all the hub-hub you can only now and then distinguish some little Christian word.

"Why do you not cut his tongue?" observed Cyrino.

"Because there is none to cut," retorted Pereira. "He was born without any. But he is a little devil who runs all over this Sertão from end to end, and at any hour of the day or night. Is not that the truth, Tico?"

The dwarf nodded his head, and glanced with an air of complacency at Cyrino.

"But is he a son of any of your people here?"

"Não, Senhor. His mother lives on the banks of the Rio Sucuriu, about a hundred and sixty miles from here, and he trots backwards and forwards from there to here in an instant, stopping awhile at the houses on the way, where every one knows him and receives him with pleasure, for he is a little

---

[16]It is customary with some of the lower classes of Brazilian peasants to file their teeth, making them pointed. The fashion is derived from the aboriginal natives of the country. (Note, Transl.)

CHAPTER VI: INNOCENCIA.

bicho who would harm no one. He remains here two, three, or more weeks, and then will disappear as suddenly as a startled woodland deer, and return to the home of his mother. He is a sort of little dog for 'Nocencia. Is it not so, Tico?"

The mute made an affirmative sign, and as he pointed towards the young woman an expression of delight spread over the queer face.

Pereira, after giving all these explanations, which the dwarf appeared to receive with satisfaction, observed, as he turned towards, or rather stooped over him:

"Go you to the big 'curral,' and gather me a large handful of leaves of the bitter orange—those from the tree close to the gate."

The little man showed by expressive gestures that he understood, and went away running.

Cyrino was about leaving the room, though not without casting a last lingering glance at the place where reposed the invalid, when Pereira called him.

"Oh, doctor, 'Nocencia wants some water, will it do her any harm?"

"Have you any sweet limes here?" he inquired.

"No end of them, and of the best."

"Then let your daughter have as many as she cares for."

Pereira, having comfortably arranged the coverings of the girl, then joined Cyrino, who had stopped at the doorway to glance at the first stars of the night.

"Do you think, doctor," inquired the Mineiro, in a somewhat tremulous voice, "there is any danger from what that little angel suffers?"

"None, absolutely none," responded Cyrino. "You will see that two days hence your daughter will have nothing the matter with her."

"These fevers are cruel things. When they do not knock over a Christian, they often make him miserable for entire years. I do not wish my daughter to become pallid nor ugly, for when young women are ill they are not attractive. Ah! I was forogetting—the sweet limes are wanted."

Pereira stepped out into the yard, and placing his hands to his mouth, called in a loud voice, "Oh! Tico!"

A prolonged cry responded at some distance.

The Mineiro uttered a modulated whistle, an Indian method of signalling, and then called for the limes.

There ensued a few moments of silence, after which the dwarf appeared running, and, approaching Pereiro, he showed by signs that he had not well heard the message.

"Some sweet limes immediately! 'Nocencia is thirsty."

The dwarf flew away like an arrow, and quickly disappeared amidst the dark shadows of the orange-trees.

CHAPTER VII: THE NATURALIST.

Night stole onwards, serene and brilliant. Innumerable stars scintillated with radiant gleams in the pure dark blue vault of the heavens, and spread over the wide ribbon of the Sertão road a soft and mystical clearness.

By the position of the stars it should be nearly midnight; nevertheless, at that dead hour—when only the wild animals of the desert wander in search of their food—two men were seen slowly wending their way along the main road, one on foot and the other was mounted on a lean and travel-worn mule.

The pedestrian appeared to be an attendant, for, with a formidable thick staff in hand, he was driving before him a long-eared baggage mule, laden with a pile of boxes and trunks.

The mounted traveller, with his body "all of a heap," his legs extended, his feet stuck out, and his head drooping upon his chest, seemed to be buried in sleep or in some profound cogitation. A tall and slender man, he had a round face, very prominent "gooseberry or goggle" eyes, a small retrousée nose, and tawny hair, beard, and moustache. His outward garments were those usually worn by travellers in Brazil, viz., buff leather top-boots, a loose cotton coat, and a broad-brimmed Chili straw hat with the brim turned down. But in addition to these common-place necessaries, he carried, suspended to a belt slung across his chest, some four or five little cases of glasses or special instruments of some kind, and in his hand a slender rod with a sack of thin rose-coloured gauze at one end.

The attendant, a middle-aged mulatto, ordinary and stupid in physiognomy, seemed, by the impatient way in which he alternately abused and thrashed his pack animal, to be by no means contented with the circumstances under which we have made his acquaintance.

The little troop proceeded on its way in the order that we have indicated, the loaded mule in front followed closely by the irritable driver, and finally by the absorbed or drowsy traveller on the lean and hungry steed.

At last, there happened an occasion when, in spite of strong and forcible expressions of language from the driver, the baggage mule appeared to wish to lodge a formal protest against the treatment that, so much beyond his customary hours of work, he now received, and firmly planting his hoofs in the sand he suddenly refused to proceed. This reluctance to further movement provoked a perfect shower of blows, the sounds of which, mingled with the cries of the attendant, echoed far away.[17]

During: some few moments the rider, who had now halted his mule, waited patiently, hoping that the pack animal would be convinced of its folly and proceed on its way.

"Júque," at last he said in broken Portuguese, and with a strong guttural accent which denoted his Teutonic origin, "if a cudgelling falls on your back like that, you love it, eh?"

---

[17]The translator cannot very well put into equivalent English the Portuguese Billingsgate of the driver—it would be too "shocking." Suffice it to say, that the mule was declared to be the personal property of his Satanic Majesty; that a thousand rays of lightnings might strike the animal with their full effect, was fervently desired; it was asserted that the poor animal would be irretrievably condemned to eternal punishment; and, finally, it was earnestly requested that the animal might suddenly be exploded by some unseen power.

CHAPTER VII: THE NATURALIST.

The man, to whom had been given the name of Júque, a familiar corruption of José, turned hastily to the speaker, and shouted:

"Look you, Mochu, this is a bicho without any shame, and ought to die under a cudgel. This life does not suit me, I—"

"But, Júque," replied the German, with unalterable calmness, "who knows but what the cargo is wounding the poor creature?"

"Nonsense," cried out the man. "It is only the obstinacy of the beast. I know this old goodfor-nothing," and, raising his staff, he delivered such a terrific blow on the hind-quarters of the animal, that it snorted with pain.

"Júque," observed the other, in the same monotone of voice, "who knows but what in front of him there is some fallen tree or a rock that will not allow him to go on?"

"Rock, Mochu? A hammering on the head until it splits is what this thief wants."

"See, Júque," insisted the German.

"Oh, Mochu!"

"Still, see."

The man went grumbling from behind his animal.

In front of it he soon chanced to tread upon the broken branch that Pereira had placed on the ground as a signal to the attendants of Cyrino to there leave the main road.

"Wah!" he exclaimed, in great surprise, "some one has been here and made a sign not to go on ahead."

"Did I not tell you," replied the horseman, in a somewhat triumphant voice. "Donkeys have reason; there must be some obstacle further on."

"But in the town," contested José, "did they not say that the road always leads straight on without any one interruption?"

"They said that in the town," confirmed the other.

"Well then?"

"Well then?" retorted the German.

Some seconds of silence ensued, presently broken by the horseman observing with the same imperturbable serenity, and as though he was finding an explanation extremely natural:

"In the town many people not know road, and— —"

"May a thousand millions of diabos," interrupted the man and shouting aloud, "seize those who have the liking to thus wander through these woods of inferno for so many wasted hours! True enough said I to Mochu, 'Nobody travels like this.' This is a real calamity, a plague."

"Júque," interrupted the master in his turn, "is to howl like a condemned soul the way to get ahead? Rather, look you, and see if about here there is not some by-road."

The other obeyed, and without difficulty found the lane leading to the abode of Pereira.

"Here it is, Mochu. Here it is," he joyfully announced. "Here is a trail that leaves the road and leads to some house close by." Suddenly altering his tone he observed in a sad voice, "Close by! It may be a good league before we get there."

"Ah! I no tell you!" responded the German. "Now drive the mule slowly, for he will go like the wind."

And really the poor mule seemed to be quite gratified with the victory its animal intelligence had obtained, for it proceeded along the new route with vigorous paces.

The true reason of its satisfaction was, that it had been so long a time since the poor beast had quenched its thirsty that, obstinate and crafty as are usually those of its species, its keen senses had been irresistibly attracted by the scent and sound of the rippling water of the stream where the animals of Cyrino and Pereira had refreshed themselves.

CHAPTER VIII: THE MIDNIGHT GUESTS.

It was not very long before the two nocturnal travellers heard the furious barking of the dogs on the premises of Pereira, announcing the approach of some one to the house under their care.

"Some ranch is close by, Mochu," observed the attendant; "at last, we shall rest to-day. But what a noise the dogs make! They are capable of swallowing us alive while some one comes to see who we are. Safa! What a row! Oh, I say, Mochu, you ought to go on in front, and lead the way."

"You," responded the German, "go and beat them with your staff."

"Not if I know it," retorted José, with energy. "That is not in the agreement. Who is mounted should go in front, now above all. Well! well! what next, I wonder?" After muttering to himself for a moment, he suddenly exclaimed, "Ah! wait, I have just thought of something. The son of the old 'un is useful after all." And saying these words, he at once sprang on to the back of the mule, which, on feeling that unexpected addition to its load, halted for some seconds, and, with a dull neigh, endeavoured to enter a protest.

"Júque," observed the German, and, without the slightest alteration in his voice, "like that, the mule break him back, then he die, and you have to carry the cargo on your shoulders."

The man intended to open a discussion on the subject, but by this time they had arrived in front of the house, where the

CHAPTER VIII: THE MIDNIGHT GUESTS.

furious onslaught of the dogs justified the precautionary measures of José, who, safely curled up behind the baggage, commenced to cry out like one possessed.

"Oh! House there! Eh! Halloa there! Somebody! Halloa! friends!"

This caused the dogs to bark and yelp even more furiously, so much so that Cyrino's men in the ranch close by awakened and drew together, saying:

"What the diabo is this? Have we a visit of Lobishomens?" (mythical wolf-men).

At this moment the door of the house opened, and Cyrino appeared followed by Pereira, who with his right hand sheltered a candle from the night breeze.

"Who comes here?" clamoured both at the same time.

"A friend and traveller," responded the German, in a strong and sympathetic voice as he approached the light and prepared to dismount. "Is the Senhor the master of this house?" he inquired.

"He himself is here," responded Pereira, raising the candle above his head in order to throw a better light about him.

"Very well," replied the new arrival. "I wish for a lodging for myself and my servant, but I must ask pardon for arriving so late."

José approached also, and at once prepared to unload the mule.

"But," observed Cyrino, "what is the Senhor doing travelling at this hour of the night?"

"Let the man enter," interrupted Pereira, "he will explain as he finds convenient. Anyhow, meu Senhor, dismount. Welcome, whoever comes under the roof that is mine."

"Thank you, thank you!" exclaimed the stranger effusively, and, tendering a huge hand, he grasped those of Cyrino and Pereira so vigorously that the bones of their fingers audibly crackled.

On entering the room he, amidst the looks of surprise of those about him, at once proceeded to remove from his breast the belt and its appendages, and to methodically arrange them on the table.

And truly, that queer figure with the "goggle eyes" as seen by the flickering light of the candle, was well worthy of observation. His legs and arms were very long, his body as correspondingly short, and his hair was so fair that it was nearly white.

"Is it some wizard?" Cyrino whispered to Pereira.

"Nonsense!" promptly responded the latter. "A man so pretty, so well dressed?"

At this moment José entered the room with a trunk on his shoulder, and after depositing it in the least dark corner of the room, he considered it his duty to define, without further delay, the quality and importance of the person whom he served as master.

"This Senhor," said he, addressing Cyrino and pointing to the German, "'is a doctor."

"Doctor?" exclaimed Cyrino contemptuously.

"Yes, but not one to cure illnesses. He is a German, from foreign parts, and has come all the way from the city of S. Sebastian of Rio de Janeiro to hunt insects and spike

CHAPTER VIII: THE MIDNIGHT GUESTS.

butterflies."

"Butterflies?" interrupted Pereira, with surprise.

"Exactly so, all the way he has been catching little bichos. Look you! That sack there that we bring— —"

"My attendant is a great talker," the naturalist tranquilly and slowly observed. "Senhor, pray have a little patience with him. Go away, Júque, and cease thy chatter."

"No," protested Pereira, prompted by feelings of curiosity. "It is as well to know with whom we treat. Then the Senhor comes here to kill insects? But whatever for? Virgem Santissima!"

"What for?" retorted the attendant, resting his hands in his waist belt. "The patron and I have already sent to his country more than ten great boxes crammed full."

"What is the Senhor called?" asked Pereira, addressing the German, who meanwhile had faced the wall to contemplate a huge dark-coloured moth he held in his hand.

"Júque," said he, without attending to the interrogation, "give me a pin, quickly; one of the big ones."

With a glance of importance José whispered to Cyrino, "Ha! ha! We have some stories to tell. You shall see soon."

The naturalist, in possession of the pin, drove it, with a steady and practised hand, through the body of the insect, which thereupon commenced to convulsively flap its wings and spin round its pivot.

"The cork! the cork!" the patron clamoured. "Quick, Júque."

José satisfied the request after opening a small case, where twenty or thirty beautiful insects were already pinned in rows.

"It is a 'Saturnia,' and not very common," murmured the German, as he pinned his specimen with the others, and dropped on it a little chloroform from a small flask he carried in one of the many pockets of his jacket.

"The Senhor is a travelling zoologist, is he not?" inquired Cyrino after watching the operation.

The German raised his head with surprise at the question, and responded with a pleased expression:

"Sim, Senhor! Sim, Senhor! How is it that you knew? Travelling zoologist! Sim, Senhor. I see that you are a well-informed man. Very good, very good!"

"Ah! He also is a doctor," said Pereira, with a certain pride at having in his house a guest of such a scientific calibre.

"Oh, indeed! Doctor? Doctor? Very good, very good. A doctor who cures, no?"

"Sim, Senhor," Cyrino responded gravely.

"Ah! ah! very good."

Pereira, however, returned to the charge. "But tell me, Senhor, how are you called?"

"Meyer," returned the German. "Your servant."

"Maia?" inquired the Mineiro.

"No, Meyer. I am from Saxony, in Germany."

"Ah! That is probably the same as Maia in his country," observed Pereira, lowering his voice.

The attendant José, without the least ceremony, now joined in the conversation. "This Mochu," said he, "comes here from far away in foreign parts, all for the sake of these butterflies, and

CHAPTER VIII: THE MIDNIGHT GUESTS.

he earns a lump of money in the business, I — —"

"Júque," interrupted his master, "go and put the animals in the pasture."

"No," said Pereira, "leave them loose in the yard until daybreak, there are enough heads of corn lying about there to keep them occupied for some time."

"Well, that is what I have done," replied the man. "I am a Carioca[18] of Rio de Janeiro, my name is José Pinho, and I accompany this German, who is a very good sort of man."

"Really?" said Pereira, gazing with interest at Meyer, who, nodding his head and glaring with his protuberant eyes, confirmed the statement of his man by uttering a deep and guttural affirmative which echoed throughout the room.

"There is one thing about him, however, continued José," and that is, he is obstinate as a mule. As I am always telling the Mochu, this habit of his of travelling at night is a stupid and useless fatigue; and a poor beggar like me has to trot along in the dark like a ghost from the other world. But there, he only says that is the best way to travel. Cruz!"

"Now, Senhor Maia," said Pereira, "'just make yourself at home in this room as if it were your own. If you want a hammock — —"

"Much obliged, much obliged, but my trunks serve me for a bed, so pray do not trouble yourself."

"Then to-morrow we will have a chat," concluded Pereira, contentedly rubbing his hands at the prospect of enjoying his chief diversion. And really, the company promised him some

---

[18]Carioca is a term applied to a native of Rio de Janeiro.—

[Transl.]

fine opportunities for his volubility, especially with José Pinho, a son of the metropolis, Rio de Janeiro, and who appeared to be a talker of rare power.

"Well then," said Pereira, opening the door to retire, "I hope you will all sleep well for the rest of the night. Wah!" he exclaimed, on glancing at the sky. "Doctor, it has already passed midnight, the Southern Cross is already on its side."

Cyrino, who meanwhile had returned to his wooden couch, immediately sprang to his feet, and, hastily drawing on his boots, took from the table some small packets he had prepared beforehand.

"Never mind," said he, "I have everything ready, and we will administer the remedy at once. Go and have some coffee ready in a cup, and awaken your daughter if she is asleep, as she probably is from the effects of the sudorific."

Pereira, with the candle in his hand, went his way accompanied by Cyrino, and, as before, they made the circuit of the house in order to reach the door giving access to the quarters of the family.

The German and his man were thus left in complete darkness, both, however, already reposing, one on his trunks with a small portmanteau for a pillow, the other on the mule's girths spread open on the floor.

"Oh! Mochu," inquired José, with his mouth full of something, "are you already shod?"

"Shod?" replied Meyer. "Now, what do you mean?"

"I asked if you had already nailed the sleep."

"Well, Júque, if I talk how can I be asleep?"

CHAPTER VIII: THE MIDNIGHT GUESTS.

"I say, wouldn't you like to munch a bit?"

"What? To eat?"

"Of course."

"Oh! Exactly what I was just thinking about."

"Well, I am grinding away you see. Would you like some?"

"What can you give me?"

"Rapadura[19] and crushed maize. It is first-rate, I can tell you."

"Then, Júque, pass me a mouthful."

The man willingly arose, and, groping in the dark for the figure of his master, and after knocking against the table and tumbling over various objects with which the floor was strewed, he finally succeeded in encountering one of the feet of his "patrão," to whom he delivered a paper full of the crushed maize and a piece of the coarse sugar—a light supper which was soon partaken of with satisfaction by the good man from Saxony.

---
[19]Rapadura, a compressed block of coarse brown sugar.

CHAPTER IX: THE REMEDY.

Innocencia was already awake when Cyrino entered her room. The father seated himself by the head of the bed, while at his feet Tico, the dwarf, reclined on the skin of a huge jaguar.

"Well," inquired the doctor, as he felt the pulse of the invalid, "how do you feel now?"

"Better," she responded.

"Very well. It is very satisfactory that the Dona is so tranquil. This ague is nothing at all when it is attacked early and has had no time to affect the blood. But when it gets a good hold of one, not even the demonio himself can do anything with it. Where is the coffee?"

"It will be here directly," replied Pereira, "Stay, I will go and fetch it myself. That Maria Conga is quite turning into a sloth. Come and sit here and wait for me an instant."

Rising from the stool, and before leaving the room, he made Cyrino occupy the vacant seat. The young man thus again found himself placed by the side of the young woman, on whose delicate features the flickering rays of the candle shed a soft light. The doctor contemplated his patient with an expression so evidently charged with tender admiration and even rapture, that the restless eyes of the dwarf sparkled even in the obscurity with a truly malevolent gleam.

The head of Innocencia reposed on the pillow, and, to still the heart's flutter that she experienced on finding herself the object of such close observation, she feigned to sleep. The beautiful eyelids at least were closed, but her heart beat tumultuously, and, occasionally, a slight rosy blush would

CHAPTER IX: THE REMEDY.

momentarily replace the pallor of her face.

Pereira yet delayed, and Cyrino, with fixed gaze and a meditative physiognomy somewhat pale betraying his inward commotion, ceased not to feast his eyes in admiration of the beauty of his new patient.

Once she half opened her eyes and shyly threw a glance which encountered that of the youth—a rapid, instantaneous glance that penetrated to her heart and caused a tremor to thrill the beauteous form.

Without knowing why or wherefore her lips trembled, and she shivered as though a cold rigour had seized her.

"Have you fever?" inquired Cyrino, in a low voice.

"I don't know," she responded.

"Let me examine the pulse," and taking her hand as he leaned over her, he tenderly pressed it in his own, and retained it there in spite of the faint efforts she occasionally made to withdraw it.

Pereira now entered. Innocencia quickly closed her eyes, and Cyrino, hastily regaining his former position, pressed a finger to his lips to indicate silence.

"Hush-sh! She is sleeping," he whispered.

"Dear, dear!" replied Pereira, in the same low tone. "That stupid Maria Conga upset the coffeepot and another lot had to be made. Did I delay very long?"

"No," responded Cyrino, in all sincerity.

"But now," observed Pereira, "we must wake up the little one."

"There is no alternative but to do so."

The father approached the bedside and called softly, "'Nocencia, 'Nocencia."

As she did not reply, he gently shook her shoulder until she opened her eyes with a startled glance.

"Apre! What asleep!" remarked the kind old man. "It was only an instant ago that I left her! Vamos! 'Nocencia, it is time for the medicine.'"

Cyrino mixed the quinine in the coffee. "Look, Dona! I want you to take this all at once, and then have some sweet limes."

"Is it then very nasty?" she somewhat petulantly inquired.

"It is bitter, but in an instant the taste will pass away."

"Papa," objected the young- girl, "I don't want it, I don't want it."

"Now, my own little darling, do not be afraid, you know it has to be. To-morrow you will be all right, won't she, doctor?"

"Certainly, if she takes the medicine."

"And when I go to the town, I will bring you something pretty

CHAPTER IX: THE REMEDY.

—some jewellery—there—do you hear that, eh?"

"Nhor-sim."

"Go, Tico," added the Mineiro, turning to the dwarf, "go quickly and fetch a sweet lime; there in the kitchen are some already peeled."

"Now take this. Dona," implored Cyrino in his turn, as hie held the cup to the lips of his beautiful patient.

She raised her eyes appealingly to him, but resolutely grasping the cup, she swallowed the nauseous draught at a gulp, gave a shudder of disgust, and sought relief in the delicate flavour of the prescribed fruit.

"There now," exclaimed Pereira, "the fear was worse than the reality; you took the dose in a twinkling."

"To-morrow morning, or, better still, at daybreak, she must have another dose, and then the Dona can get up."

"Yet another?" protested Innocencia, with a gesture of petulance.

"Yes, Dona, it is absolutely necessary," replied the amorous doctor, softening, by a tender inflection of his voice, the severity of the prescription.

"Certainly it is," corroborated Pereira.

"Afterwards the Dona must refrain from any fresh meat for a whole month, neither take any milk, green vegetables, eggs, or maize flour. She must partake only of thoroughly-cured sun-dried beef, and rice with very little salt, and, above all, take coffee with only a little sugar in it.[20]

---

[20]This regime for fever convalescents is religiously observed throughout the Sertão of Brazil.

"These instructions," added Pereira, "must be followed with the greatest attention."

"Now I hope you will sleep well, and do not be frightened if you feel a singing in your ears or even become a little deaf, for that is only the effect of the medicine, and it is a good sign."

"These doctors know everything," murmured Pereira, as he hastily crossed himself.

Cyrino, before retiring from the room, on the plea of once more examining the pulse of his patient, failed not to take her hand in his and grasp it with a tender pressure.

A sound man he entered the room to cure an invalid, but he left it with the newly-acquired infirmity of love-sickness.

When he returned to the guest's room he sought sleep in vain, and tossed restlessly on his hard couch until the first gleams of dawn, without having once obtained a moment's repose. That face he had gazed upon, those eyes whose shy glances he had perceived, that vision of the alabaster neck, the shadowed outline of the graceful form—all these formed salient points in the memory of that harmonious array of beauteous charms as seen by the fitful light of the candle, and served to fatally plunge him into that abyss sown with torments called a "passion."

The first rays of dawn stole into the chamber of the guests, and the silence of the hour was only disturbed by the still restless movements of Cyrino on his hard couch, by the crow of a cock, or by the heavy breathing of Meyer, echoing and keeping time to the resonant snoring of the garrulous José Pinho.

CHAPTER X: THE LETTER OF RECOMMENDATION.

When Meyer opened his eyes in the mornings heperceived Cyrino already up and occupied in arranging the contents of a small trunk.

"Oh!" he exclaimed admiringly, "the Senhor is indeed an early riser."

"It is true," Cyrino somewhat sadly replied.

"And Júque yet sleeps! He is a man, that Júque. He seems more like an armadillo than a human being. All day long I have to keep waking him up."

And adapting his practice to his words, the phlegmatic master proceeded to arouse the servant, who, after a prodigious amount of awful yawns, groans, and stretching of limbs, at last sat up on the hide on which he had slept, and commenced to rub his puffy and sleepy eyes.

"God be with your worships," said he at last in the interval of two terrific yawns. "Oh, Mochu! you have robbed me of the best of my sleep. I was just dreaming that I had returned to Rio de Janeiro and was following a band of music in the Largo de Rocio. Do you know the Largo de Rocio?" he inquired of Cyrino.

"No."

"Sheeh! What a square it is! Eh, Mochu? It— —" Another yawn impeded the coming description of the famed square.

"Júique," exclaimed Meyer joyfully, "the day is clear and bright; we shall be able to collect at least twenty new butterflies."

"How much will Mochu give me if I capture twenty-five?"

"Five-and-twenty?" repeated the German doubtfully.

"Yes, five-and-twenty, and even more, six-and-twenty. Say, how much will you give?"

"Oh! I give you two milreis."

"It is done. I close the bargain. I am always thus; as bread is bread and cheese is cheese, so certain am I that they call me José Pinho, your servant, Carioca by birth, christened in the parish of Lagoa, out there by the way of Broco, and — —"

"Now," interrupted Meyer, "go and fetch some water for a wash, and find the soap and comb in the trunk."

"Now, look you, doctor," continued the servant, still seated on the floor and turning to Cyrino, "this life of mine is six hundred diabos. We left Rio more than two years ago. Eh, Mochu?"

"Two-and-twenty months," replied the methodical Meyer.

"Very well. Now, all this time we have just been on the tramp as though we were doing a job of penitence. And not only that, not a bit of it. Every day we march at least thirty-six miles, running here, there, backwards and forwards, tumbling about, and all in search of the flying bichos."

"Júque," Meyer attempted to observe, "look you — —"

"Well, it is as I say," proceeded José Pinho. "I am now just mad against such tomfoolery. I can't imagine why Nosso Senhor created such a heap of useless creatures. Well, he only knows. As to myself, I would, if I could, put fire to all the maggots, for from maggots come out all these 'innesects' that

CHAPTER X: THE LETTER OF RECOMMENDATION.

are filling up worlds of places. But look you, doctor, there, in the country of this man—poor fellow, he is a very good sort you know, and I think very much of him—why, these bichos are worth oven more than gold dust. Also, if the Mochu did not like me very much, I would not put up with what I have to bear. Such another as he you will not meet, não, Senhor—one who has so much patience. No, there are not two of them. I know."

During this flood of words Meyer went himself to procure in his trunk the requisite soap and comb, and showing these objects to the speaker, he energetically vociferated:

"Shut up, Júque! Shut up, chatterbox! Go, fetch some water, or I will not take you with me to the woods to-day."

With many mutterings to himself, and taking a large zinc basin from amidst the baggage, José Pinho went away to obey the order.

"That man," presently observed Meyer, in apology for his servant, "is a very good fellow, faithful and honest, but an awful talker. But to me he is invaluable, for he catches butterflies with great dexterity."

The man entering at the moment thus heard his own praises. Therefore, with an air of grave importance, he placed the great basin on the ground in front of Meyer, who, after removing his spectacles, squatted by its side.

The legs of the German were so long in comparison to his body, that when he bent his head over the water his knees were on a level with his shoulder.

The ablution occupied some minutes, and the hair was still glued to his skull and the water yet dripping from his long locks, when Pereira entered.

The appearance of the naturalist was grotesque in the extreme; nevertheless, so varied is the appreciation of every one of us, so capricious the judgment of the senses, that the Mineiro, approaching Cyrino, said to him in a low voice:

"Do you not observe, my friend, how fine a figure is this foreigner? So stately he is, and what eyes he has! Any woman would lose her heart for the sake of this big bicho. Well, Senhor Maia," he continued in a loud voice, as he interpolated his idea of masculine beauty, "how have you passed the night?"

"Ah! Senhor Pereira! Pardon me for not seeing you, I am without my spectacles, but wait an instant and I will talk to you," and still dripping wet, he ran for his glasses. "Now I am all right," he added, as he placed them before his salient eyes. "My good friend, I slept like one without sins."

"Then," observed Cyrino, "I should have them in abundance, for, from midnight until now, I have not closed an eye."

"This is the return of some *amor*," replied Pereira, laughing, and clapping his guest on the shoulder.

Cyrino trembled visibly.

"Yes, you are a young man, and doubtless have left some sweetheart behind you up there in Minas, and now and then her memory upsets the heart. Ah! It is just the age for it, you know."

"That's it, most probably," added Meyer, with all gravity.

"Now, is it not so?" insisted Pereira. "Now, confess—it will do you no harm—is it not really a return of *amor*?"

"I—I will swear," stammered Cyrino.

CHAPTER X: THE LETTER OF RECOMMENDATION.

"Oh, if it is," observed José Pinho, who considered he ought to join in the conversation, "I, in Rio Janeiro——"

The German calmly turned towards his follower and cut short any further remarks of his.

"Júque," said he, "go at once and see after the mules, and don't you meddle when white people are talking with your patrão."

As the man was about to retort—

"Go, go," continued his ever-serene master, "your discussion never serves for anything."

José muttered something, but went away grumbling to himself.

Meyer thought it right to again apologise for his man.

"A good fellow," said he, "a good fellow, but an awful talker."

"But now, really, do tell me," earnestly inquired Pereira, stepping back a pace and expressing on his face the anxiety of one who desired to solve a doubtful problem. "Is it actually true that the Senhor is wandering all over these Sertãos just to stick 'innesects'?"

"Certainly," responded Meyer, with some enthusiasm. "In my country they are very valuable for purposes of science, and for placing in museums and collections. I am travelling by order of my government, and already I have forwarded many cases all full. They are very precious indeed."

"Now, just think of that," exclaimed Pereira, aghast with astonishment. "Whoever could imagine that one could ever go a hunting these bichos? Cruz! A man like this—a doctor—to go a running about after fireflies and other little bichos of the woods just like some boy a chasing the cicadas! Well! Well! One learns a lot in this world? Now look you, Senhor, if I had not a family, I would be quite capable of going with you to these worlds away about here, for I always like to mix with people of quality. That's my nature. Who knows me, knows that is so— —"

"How goes the invalid?" inquired Cyrino, distractedly, interrupting that cataract of words.

"Truly, I am very contented. She took another dose, and seems now to be nearly well, and already looks like another person. The Senhor really performed a miracle."

"Under favour of Deos, the Virgin Purissima and all the Saints of Heaven," added Cyrino, with all modesty.

"Don't you cure?" inquired Pereira of Meyer.

"No, Senhor. I am a doctor in philosophy of the University of Leipzig, and— —"

"Is that the name of a bicho?" interrupted Pereira.

"No, Senhor. It is a city."

"No one would have thought it. But, Senhor Maia," continued Pereira, as he pointed towards Cyrino. "There stands one with whom the fevers won't play the fool. Eh?"

"Ah!" exclaimed the German, opening yet more his prominent eyes. "I am very happy to know such a distinguished notability. In places like this they are very rare— —"

"Ah! Are they not?" exclaimed Pereira. "Fortunately he arrived here just in time to put the child on her feet, a daughter of mine—and— —"

The face of Cyrino flushed, and with difficulty he suppressed

CHAPTER X: THE LETTER OF RECOMMENDATION.

the emotion he experienced at her mention, and with a grave air he ejaculated, "Pray don't mention it, Senhor Pereira. The case was a very simple one. Merely an ordinary fever common to the rainy season. I saw at once what was necessary to be done; a mild sudorific and two or three doses of quinine, and the thing is finished."

Meyer followed these therapeutical indications with his eyes fixed upon the speaker. Afterwards he turned to Pereira, and, with an emphatic nod of his head, expressed his approbation by saying:

"Good doctor! Good doctor!"

From that moment Cyrino experienced a decided sympathy for the German; and Pereira, seeing the friendly disposition of the men towards each other, and one which he had been instrumental in establishing between two such evidently great savants, felt very much gratified to have this opportunity of sheltering both of them at the same time under his humble roof.

"Then," said the Mineiro, recommencing to touch upon the butterfly question, "withal, your government pay you very well. Eh, Senhor Maia?"

"Sufficiently; and all the authorities aid me very much. I have many letters—letters of introduction. Here, would you like to see them? Júque! Júque!" he clamoured, forgetting that the man had left the room, "come here! Ah, I forgot that he has gone to water the animals. Never mind, I will show you directly."

Taking from amidst his baggage a small waterproof-covered box, he opened it and produced therefrom a bundle of letters carefully numbered and neatly tied with tape.

"This one is for Miranda, in Mato Grosso," he announced, as he turned over the letters. "This one is for Cuyaba, this for Diamantina. These others here are letters that I shall have to return to the writers, for I could not find the people to whom they were addressed."

"Are there many of them?" inquired Pereira.

"Three or four. Here is one for Senhor João Manoel Quaresma, in Oliveira; another for Senhor Quintana, in Pitanguy; this one is for Senhor Martinho dos Santos Pereira, in Piumhy——"

"Eh! What!" almost screamed the Mineiro, greatly astonished. "Read that name again; read."

Meyer obeyed.

"But that name is mine!" exclaimed Pereira excitedly. "That letter is for me."

"Wha-a-at!" stammered the German, in surprise. "Now that is very curious."

"It is me—me!" boisterously shouted the Mineiro. "That is clear. Whoever wrote that letter thought that I yet lived in Piumhy, for I never told any one where I moved to. Open the letter without fear. Oh, Senhora Sant'Anna! What a day it is, surely! Who would have thought it? A letter! You can read it, Senhor Maia. I am all afire to know who wrote me—Martinho dos Santos Pereira, of Piumhy! Yes, that's me; no doubt of it. There are not two of us. Just see the name—the name only—of whoever has sent me the letter."

The German after some scrupulous hesitation broke the seal, and, glancing his eyes over the letter, he slowly read aloud the signature:

"Francisco dos Santos Pereira."

CHAPTER X: THE LETTER OF RECOMMENDATION.

"Chiquinho!"[21] exclaimed the Mineiro, in the height of joy. "It is my brother Chiquinho, whom I long ago thought to be dead. May Nosso Senhor preserve him for many years! Oh, Chiquinho! Did any one ever see anything like this? What strange things happen in this world! Eh, Senhor Cyrino? Who would have thought that this man who arrived here in the middle of last night would bring in his trunk a letter from my brother—he whom I have not seen for more than forty years? Well, well, what changes there are in this world! What—let me see—ah, yes, it was in 1819—no, in 20. But there, read me the letter; let's see what Chiquinho says to me. Poor old chap, he must be pretty old now. Out of all the family he was the most sensible; he was also the oldest. Oh, Senhor, you are indeed welcome to this house! Whoever brings me notice of my family— —"

Meyer interrupted this torrent of effusion, which promised to be without end, by commencing to slowly read, or rather spell out, the contents of the communication, for the queer characters of the letters sometimes obliged him to twist and turn the paper, hold it close to his eyes, or try to decipher it in one position or another.

"Martinho," said the letter, "I send you these ill-traced lines only to hear of your health and to tell you that the bearer is a Senhor of great learning, and who goes to the wild Sertão travelling and studying the countries. He came to me from Rio do Janeiro, strongly recommended. I ask you to accommodate him, not as any casual passer-by, but as if he were I in person, your eldest brother, and the head of our family— —"

"Poor brother!" exclaimed Pereira, half crying.

"He is a man," Meyer continued to read, "of great education.

---

[21]Little Frank.

Adeus, Martinho. I am settled here in Mato do Pio, on a small farm. I have five children—three males and two females; these last are married, and have some long time ago given me grandchildren. My health and strength are yet good. It is more than eight years since I received any news of you. Do you know that Roberto died in Paranan——?"

"Roberto? Ah, poor fellow!" Pereira interrupted, in a moved tone of voice, and suddenly, as the memories of his boyhood flashed across his mind, his eyes filled with tears.

"And without more," concluded Meyer, "adeus. May you be happy, and adeus. Your brother, Francisco dos Santos Pereira."

"Well, really," said Pereira, somewhat affected, as he tendered his hand to the German, "the Senhor has indeed filled me with joy. Clasp this hand, and if ever it is raised, even to disturb a hair of your head, or against any one of your family—no matter what may be the offence—then may it be destroyed by Deos, who now hears me!"

"Thank you, Senhor Pereira," said the other with animation as he returned the clasp of the hand.

"Sim Senhor," continued the Mineiro. "This letter I value more than one from the Emperor who governs Brazil. That is what I say, Senhor Maia."

"Meyer," observed the German, emphasising the last syllable, "Meyer."

"Ah! True. It is necessary to translate: Meyer, Meyer. Ah! now I have got hold of the thing. But as I was about to say, this house is yours. My brother, my eldest brother, told me to receive you as if you were he himself, Chico. Well, so shall it be. You shall be just one of our family. Any one can see that is

CHAPTER X: THE LETTER OF RECOMMENDATION.

what he means. I understood at once. If I did not, I should be very stupid, and by favour of Deos no one can say that of me. The Senhor will dispose of me as he wills, and my barn, my lands, my slaves, my cattle and every thing else, in part, or wholly, are his. Who is now speaking is no longer the owner of any one thing here, the real owner is the Senhor. My brother wrote me, that is enough. There is no need to think for a moment that I will not obey the orders of my superiors and relatives. It is just as if I had received a command from the hand of the Emperor, the son of Pedro the First, who turned out the Portuguese and raised this Empire on the field of Ipyranga, away there by S. Paulo de Piratinim; where in those days there used to be a college of priests and monks in great number, the starting place of the old pioneers who went out to distant worlds to fight the wild Indians, and hunt jaguars, and carry their standards to the banks of the Paraguay and the falls of the Parana, even extending their excursions to the Reductions[22] whence they brought away a crowd of captives in chains[23] but so many of whom died on the road that only a few hundred arrived, and so thin were they that— —"

Pereira delivered himself of all these phrases with surprising volubility, so much so that Meyer gazed at him with a blank expression of astonishment, while he waited for an interval in the torrent of words to slip in some words of thanks. It was, however, only after some moments, that he was enabled to sharply ejaculate a resonant "Thank you," and follow it up by observing:

---

[22]"Reductions" were the names given to the settlements of Indians in the care of the Jesuits in Paraguay. In 1630 there were twenty such settlements, with 70,000 inhabitants.

[23]It is reported that 140 Spaniards entered Paraguay from Brazil and attacked the "Reductions," with 1,500 Tupy Indians, all well armed and in military order, and carried away as slaves 7,000 prisoners.

"But the Senhor talks like a very cataract. Do you not get tired?"

"Tired? Not a bit," replied the Mineiro boastfully. "The people all about here are by nature only little talkers, but I—no, Senhor, for I was born and bred amongst civilised people."

CHAPTER XI: THE BREAKFAST.

Cyrino suddenly arose from the couclh on which he had been seated. "I must see about continuing my journey to-morrow," said he.

"What! doctor?" protested Pereira. "Go away already? No, that will never do. Why, you have not yet quite cured my daughter. I will pay you for your delay here, that is, if it be necessary."

"Oh, Senhor Pereira," protested the youth, "that would offend me indeed."

"Well, I pray you to pardon me, but I cannot think of allowing you to leave hero under two weeks at least."

"But——"

"Oh, bother your buts! Remember, you won't want for patients. My ranch will be visited as if it was a public house of entertainment, and the Senhor will really not be able to attend to all who come for advice. Look you! I have already sent to tell Coelho, and in a little while he will be sticking to you like a carapato. No, Senhor, you don't leave this yet awhile. Do you wish to desert 'Nocencia as she is, even yet?"

"Ah, truly," precipitately observed Cyrino.

"Well then? It is not good even to think about it. Let things remain as they are for my sake, for anyhow you will have to arrange your business here."

"Ah! That is just what I was about to mention, for I feared the trouble might inconvenience you. Once that patients begin to arrive here— —"

"They will come; remain here without any fear."

"Well, I will, then," Cyrino decided. "Just as long as you please."

"Bravo! That is capital!" exclaimed Pereira, with sincerity. "It is just what I would like. As to Senhor Maia—Meyer I mean— he will have to take root in this house."

"That cannot be, my time is all marked out by my government."

"Well, well, but you must make a long stay with us. It is a pity that the Manecão is not here, so that I might hurry up the wedding, when we would have such a festival as never was seen in these woods. But here am I with my tongue a rattling away and not even thinking that our stomachs have had nothing to-day. Breakfast ought to be ready directly. I will go and see after it."

He left the room on saying these words, and, in a few moments afterwards he returned with Maria, the old negress, carrying the table-cloth and a gourd full of farinha.

"Senhores," cried Pereira boisterously, "to-day I will breakfast with you both at this table, but listen, Senhor Meyer, after to-day you will eat with me and my daughter there inside," pointing as he spoke to the rear of the house, and, turning to Cyrino, "Well, you know," he explained, "he is now one of the family, as though he were Chiquinho himself."

The table spread, the three men gleefully seated themselves thereat.

"Look you, Senhor Meyer," said the Mineiro as he served the German, "these are the very best of beans. Mix them with the

CHAPTER XI: THE BREAKFAST.

rice and herbs, and add a few pinches of farinha."

The naturalist commenced to masticate with the slowness of a ruminating animal, occasionally interrupting the morose exercise to exclaim, "Delicious really! Very delicious!"

Cyrino eat little and maintained silence.

"In Germany," declared Meyer, contemplating a bean, "the largest beans do not attain this size. Such a breakfast as this would cost in Saxonia quite two thalers, or about two thousand five hundred reis."

Pereira interrupted him by observing with a comical gesture! "Two thousand five hundred reis? Dear me! Why, whatever sort of country is that? How do you call it?"

"Sac-sonia," responded the German, with gravity.

"Saco-sonha!" exclaimed Pereira. "I never heard tell of it; but surely, people must go about there dying of hunger?"

"According to the last statistics," replied Meyer slowly, and with many pauses, in order to introduce to his mouth enormous spoonfuls of the mixture as prescribed by his host, "it is known that in London there is a daily average of 8 deaths from starvation, in Berlin, 5, in Vienna, 4, in Paris, 2, in Pekin, 12, in Jeddo, 7, in— —"

"Ho! ho! ho!" shouted Pereira, in a tone of exultation; "then bravo for our land of Brazil, whore no one need know what hunger means; for if in the house there is nothing to eat, you have but to go to the forest for the wild honey of the Jatahy or the Mandory bees, or the cabbage of the Macaubeira, and scores of other things. That is, at least, hereabouts in these parts, because in the cities all you have to do is to spread open your hand, and lo! alms at once rain down on it. That is what I understand a country should be, anything else is a disgrace."

"Ah!" replied the German. "Brazil is indeed a very fertile and a very rich country. It provides coffee for half the world to drink, and when it has more people it will supply enough for all the globe."

"Was I not right then, eh?" exclaimed Pereira, with a glance of triumph as he clasped Cyrino by the shoulder. "You see, even these foreigners know all about us. What say you, my fellow countryman. Holloa, man! What are you silent about, half deaf and dumb like? What is it? The same old business again, eh?"

In fact, after hearing the invitation offered to Meyer to join the family circle of the household of Pereira, Cyrino had become dejected, restless, and meditative. His body remained with his host, but his mind wandered to that little room where reposed the fever-stricken maiden, yet so beautiful even with the pallor of illness.

"If the trouble is some woman," continued Pereira, "don't worry yourself about it so, nothing is more stupid. They are a kind of goods always found in abundance everywhere."

Meyer, in the midst of the exercise of his jaws, believed that his host considered the feminine sex from a statistical point of

CHAPTER XI: THE BREAKFAST.

view, and accordingly thought it advisable to enforce ideas somewhat vaguely expressed. "Certainly," said he dogmatically, "in the Slav race the proportion is two women to one man; in the Latins, of two men to one woman. In France, the proportion on the masculine side is——"

"But have you counted them?" interrupted Pereira, "Let me tell you one thing, I wont swallow Macaws."[24]

"Nor I," Meyer affirmed, with some indignation. "I know not why you now mention those bichos; if considered in the sense of game, all know that these climbers have tough flesh and—"

Pereira, who laughed immoderately at the German's misapprehension, at once explained the real sense of his expression, and continued to discuss with his methodical and polite interlocutor.

"You might talk to me for a whole year," said the Mineiro finally, "but I would not understand a tittle of your jigy-jogy 'stic-tics' and countings. Whoever removes me from the floor puts me in the woods[25] But now let us return thanks to Deus, our Saviour, for giving us this good meal."

Following his words by example, he rose to his feet, and, with clasped hands and in a low voice, he uttered the words of the grace, in which he was accompanied by his two guests.

"Now," announced Pereira, on leaving the table, "I will just have a run through the plantation, where three good-for-nothing blacks are at work, one of whom is my foreman. Afterwards I shall have to look up some neighbours to tell them of your arrival, doctor. Ah, but," he added, "I have not

---

[24] An expression of incredulousness.

[25] Pereira wished to express that unfamiliar subjects of conversation were beyond the possibility of his comprehension.

yet shown you my daughter, Senhor Meyer."

"'Your daughter!" exclaimed the German; "then have you children?"

"Sim, Senhor. Don't you remember that your person is that of my brother Chiquinho? Well, then, what greater proof of confidence and friendship can I give you? Eh, Senhor Cyrino?"

"Ah, without doubt," stammered the young man, as he endeavoured to control his confusion.

"My daughter, who is called 'Nocencia, only to-day got up from a sick-bed. She has been ill. Even now I know not that the ague has quite left her, for sometimes the body is long affected with the pest."

"That you must leave to my care," observed Cyrino hastily; "she must yet take some more quinine at midday."

"Do as you think best. Would you like to see her, Senhor Meyer?"

"Certainly, certainly," the German amiably replied.

"She is the only member of my family that I have here, besides a certain big fellow, a son of mine, who is on the road hereabouts. Then let us go. Come you also," he continued, addressing Cyrino; "a surgeon is almost one of the family."

The three men then left the room and proceeded towards the rear, or family quarters, of the premises.

CHAPTER XII: THE PRESENTATION.

After traversing a room somewhat obscurely lighted, the visitors entered an adjoining one, spacious in area, floored with red tiles, and, being without any ceiling, exposing to view the thatch and rafters of the roof above.. In a corner of this chamber, and on a bamboo sofa, was seated the daughter of the Mineiro.

Her feet rested on the skin of a huge ant-eater, on which squatted the dwarf Tico.

The beautiful girl, on seeing so many visitors, opened her great eyes wide with surprise, and attempted to rise, but the effort was unavailing, and, slightly blushing, she almost fainted with weakness.

Cyrino flew eagerly towards her. "The maiden," said he to Pereira, "is so weak that it is painful to see her."

The father approached her with Meyer, and gently taking her hands in his, he inquired, in a tender voice, "Do you feel any worse, my child?"

"Nhor-não" (No, Sir), she responded.

"Well, then, you really must not give way to such weakness. Open your eyes. Look! Here is this man," pointing to Meyer, "a German, who has brought a letter from your uncle Chico away there in Mato do Rio. I want to show him that he is now one of our own people, so I have brought him to present him to you."

She made no reply.

"Come! come! Say something. Say you have much pleasure in making his acquaintance. Say so."

Innocencia slowly and timidly repeated the words, and Meyer tendered his hand, large as the flapper of a turtle, and frank and generous as his heart.

"Pleasure, much pleasure, have I," said he, with two or three sonorous gurgles of the throat, "although I regret to see you ill. But the doctor here will soon make you well. Is it not so, Senhor Cyrino, Hein?" He uttered the last word in a tone that echoed throughout the room.

"It is advisable," said the young man, "for the Dona to take, during some days, some bark of the quina of the campos mixed with a little good wine, but where shall I now find wine? Only in the town of Sant'Anna."

"Wine?" inquired Meyer.

"Yes."

"Port wine?"

"Better still."

"Well, all is arranged. In my trunk I have a bottle of the very best, and with very much pleasure I will cede it to the daughter of my friend Pereira."

"Oh! Senhor Meyer," thankfully and effusively exclaimed Pereira. "You cannot imagine how I—"

"Oh! no, not at all, no obligation whatever. No, Senhor, your daughter is really lovely, and appears to be an equally good girl. She must naturally have such a beautiful colour that I would give anything to see her in health. What a maiden! What loveliness!"

CHAPTER XII: THE PRESENTATION.

These words, that the innocent Saxon pronounced *ex abundantia cordis*, produced extraordinary commotion in the persons who heard them.

Pereira turned pale, and his brows frowned as he threw a sidelong glance of astonishment at one who so imprudently eulogised, face to face, the beauty of his daughter. Innocencia blushed fiercely. Cyrino, almost beside himself, experienced a strange feeling of admiration; while the dwarf, half terrified, leaped up from the ant-eater rug.

Meyer did not observe the confusion of his companions, and, with his habitual sincerity, he proceeded:

"Here, in the Sertão of Brazil, exists a very bad custom of hiding from sihht the females of a household. A traveller knows not whether they are beautiful or ugly. But, on my word, Senhor Pereira, if they are all like this young woman, your daughter, it is a fact really worthy of mention. I——"

"Shall we go?" interrupted Pereira testily.

"Certainly," replied the German, and, as a parting salutation to Innocencia, he added, as he turned towards her, "I, Wilhelm Tembel Meyer, your servant, am most happy to know you as the daughter of a friend of mine, and one who captivates me with your charming face." Tendering his hand, he bowed, and then followed the Mineiro, who left the room with his face livid with anger.

"And what think you of this man?" he inquired of Cyrino, in a low voice.

"I certainly was astonished at his manner," replied the young man in the same tone.

"I hardly know how to contain myself—I—I am blinded with

rage. Oh" what a present Chico has sent me! He is a pest, is this yellow diabo. No sooner does he see a girl when he lets her have a half-dozen of soapy compliments. Bah! he must be a bad one. A good for nothing. But there, you leave me alone, I will keep an eye upon him."

"You will do well," observed Cyrino.

"Now, look you," continued Pereira, detaining his companion in order to allow Meyer to go onwards, "Am I not in a pretty mess? If it was not for that letter of my brother's, I swear that that fellow would to-day have to dance to a good cudgelling. The ruffian! Just imagine! A woman who expects a husband in a couple of days. Let us only hope that Manecão will hear nothing of this, or otherwise his knife will soon be into the rascal. Eh! just think of it, eh! Ah! Those chaps from foreign parts! Cruz! Yet there, when I first saw him—a fine pretty fellow, a thorough coxcomb—I might have known that he was a gallant after the women."

Cyrino listened in silence.

"And woman," continued the Mineiro with wrathful volubility, "is a thing so easily influenced by any foolery, that these idiots slobber over them with their flattery and nonsense. With women, I say always, you never know where you are. Ah! it was a bad hour that brought this German—and Chico above all. Eh! I must now be cautious, as—as a hunter waiting at a saltlick—and dig pitfalls so that the wild cat of the woods may not enter my fowl-house."

"He will soon be going away," said Cyrino; consolingly.

"May the demon seize him," replied Pereira, "I am just furious all over with the man."

At this moment, Meyer inopportunely returned and observed:

CHAPTER XII: THE PRESENTATION.

"Senhor Pereira, I will stop with you, perhaps, two weeks. The mules will then get strong and fat in your pasture, and meanwhile I shall make journeys on foot all about the neighbourbood to collect anything I can find. Do you hear?"

Pereira expressed a gesture of strong discontent, but, influenced by the instinct and duties of hospitality, be responded somewhat drily:

"Remain two weeks, or two months, or two years. The house is yours, I have already told you, and my word of honour once given returns no more. Who is here now is not the Senhor, you are my oldest brother himself."

Then grasping firmly the band of Cyrino, he whispered to him, "Look you, doctor, see this now! What shall I say to him? Ha! ha! ha! My Meyer, you want to play the fool with me, eh? But here also remain I. Now that I know you, not two, nor three like you, can throw dust in my eyes. Not this way you don't, 'Nocencia is the daughter of a poor man, but, thanks to Maria Santissima, she has a father with two arms and courage to defend her from the vagabonds and rovers of the road. He won't play with Manecão: that is a man, if you like, and, if he places his hand on his prey, he will crush his bones like a forest deer in the folds of an anaconda."

Meyer, however, absolutely unaware of the storm that his words had provoked, and without doubt a little disturbed in mind in thinking of the maiden he had just visited, lightly hummed between his teeth the air of a German waltz, perhaps danced with some fair countrywoman of his in a bygone period of happier associations and surroundings.

CHAPTER XIII: SUSPICIONS.

When the man of Saxony returned to the guest's room, he appeared so pleased with the treatment he had received, and with the favourable state of the weather for collecting butterflies, that he called the attention of his servant José, who, seated on a trunk, was examining the soles of his bare feet to see if some small stone had entered that thick and insensible material.

"Man!" he familiarly replied. "Mochu is very merry to-day. Has he seen any little green bird?"

"Any little green bird?" inquired Meyer. "What do you mean? I have seen no little green bird, but I have seen a very beautiful young woman."

"Ha! ha! Better still; but who is she?"

"She is the daughter of Senhor Pereira."

"I congratulate you! I congratulate you!" exclaimed José, with great indiscretion.

"Júque," rebuked the German, assuming a serious expression, "don't you be too familiar with people who are not of your class."

"But I did not say anything wrong, Mochu."

Pereira, who had also entered the room and heard these sentences, felt as if he was seated on a fire of coals. "Decidedly that guest of mine intends to irretrievably disgrace me, to thus proclaim aloud, as with a trumpet, that he has seen Innocencia, that he had conversed with her, that he had found her beautiful—her, a young woman almost a bride! Oh! what insolence! Ah, my Saints of Paradise! What prudence I require,

CHAPTER XIII: SUSPICIONS.

for any one ill-considered step may be charged with irremediable consequences."

It is necessary to penetrate the sentiments which so disturbed the Mineiro in order to appreciate the cause of the varying moods through which he passed, and to see that it was but natural that he should adopt a line of conduct full of waveringdoubts. If, on the one hand, he felt an involuntary admiration for Meyer, and surrounded him in imagination with the prestige of irresistibly attractive charms, this only served to add to the terror of having so dangerous a guest amidst his household. Yet, on the other hand, he felt himself bound by the imperious duties of hospitality, which, with the wishes of his elder brother, assumed a character almost sacred. But in antagonism to this bond of moral obligation rose up the inexorable laws of domestic circumspection, the responsibility of screening from the eyes of strangers the sanctuary of the family; for even with his great love for his daughter—she being a woman—he reposed in her not the slightest trust, especially when the supposition forced itself upon him of the sentiment which that too-seductive foreigner must naturally create in the heart of Innocencia, despite of the fact of her being already betrothed. Moreover, he foresaw the difficulty that he would have to encounter in maintaining immutable his word of honour, perhaps even at the cost of defending his honour itself. All these complex problems revolving in the mind of Pereira, showed their disturbing effect on his usually jovial face in sombre looks of uneasiness.

In order to divert the conversation which had so embittered him, he inquired of José Pinho, "For what reason do you call Senhor Meyer 'the Mochu'?"

The man from Rio do Janeiro smiled with an air of superiority, and explained without embarrassment:

"Oh! it is merely a way of speaking."

"How so?"

"Now, look here! Don't you call him 'the Senhor'?"

"Yes, I do."

"Well then, so do I, but I do it in French, that's all. Mochu means Senhor in that language."

"Ah!" replied Pereira, appearing to be convinced; "that is it then; I thought it was something else."

"Júque," observed Meyer, "get the things ready, we are going to the woods at once."

"Come with me," proposed the Mineiro in an insinuating voice. "I will show you places where there are bichos without end."

"With much pleasure," replied the German, and, turning towards his man, he continued: "Hurry, Júque. Put aside your smoke. Get ready the tin boxes, chloroform, and net. Hurry, man, hurry!"

Instigated by these words, José Pinho rushed about the room as though distraught with the perplexity of the demands.

"My glasses," added the naturalist. "The sack for the plants; the tube for the beetles. Come, come, hurry! There, I will help you." And, in his turn, he commenced to search for the required objects and prepare for the occasion. To a broad belt, which he slung across his breast, he attached two or three small leather-covered cases, one of which contained a silver cup and chain, another, a many-bladed knife. To a waist-belt he suspended a wicker-work-covered flask of aquadente, which he had purchased in passing through the town of

CHAPTER XIII: SUSPICIONS.

Sant'Anna do Paranahyba. Not content with the weight of these appendages to his person, he further added a hunting knife, a short sword, and a revolver. After making all these arrangements to his satisfaction (but to the great surprise of Pereira, and even of Cyrino), he removed his spectacles and replaced them with a pair of very large convex smoked glasses, as a protection to his eyes from the glare of the sun, against which he also armed himself with another singular protector—a broad ring of stiff white cloth lined with green, through which he passed the crown of his Chili hat, the brim serving to support the ring.

In this rig, Meyer was the most extraordinary-looking person that any Christian could meet with in any of the surrounding three hundred leagues; nevertheless, Pereira felt offended with all those preparations, which he looked on as witchcraft.

"See," he whispered to Cyrino, "how this magician is ornamenting himself! But you don't humbug me, oh, no you don't, Senhor German of my sins."

At this moment the naturalist glanced about to see if anything was yet wanting to complete his equipment. "I am ready now," he at last exclaimed, "and very anxious to get into the woods."

"The carrapatos[26] will set you a-tingling," muttered Pereira.

"Ah! My gloves," said Meyer. "Júque, look for them in No. 2 trunk in the left-hand further corner."

The servant produced a pair of well-worn capacious white woollen gloves, into which the hands of the German dived in one movement.

"Now, Sim Senhor," he exclaimed, with animation, as he

---
[26]The carrapatos are exceedingly irritating ticks which frequent the Brazilian bush.

announced his readiness for departure, and uttering a sonorous and prolonged "Humph," he seized his butterfly net, but pausing a moment and placing a finger to his brow. "Ah!" he exclaimed, "The wine, I was nearly forgetting it. The wine for your daughter, Senhor Pereira, your lovely daughter."

The Mineiro shrugged his shoulders impatiently, and observed aside to Cyrino: "He pretended to forget. Look at that now, eh! But this bicho won't throw dust in my eyes, oh, no he won't, not if I know it."

As he received the bottle of wine from the hands of José Pinho, he added aloud, "Thank you very much for your present, Senhor Meyer, but if—if you cannot spare it, the little one will have to get cured without it."

"No, no, no, no," replied the Saxon with a series of negatives that seemed as if they would have no end.

"In this world," muttered Pereira to himself, "no one drives home a charge of shot without the wadding; but with Sertanejos[27] one does not play the fool."

"This," said Cyrino, taking the bottle in his hand, "will complete the cure with certainty." Avoiding any pronunciation of the name or quality of the person whom he was treating, he added, "She ought to have a little appetite to-day, and may get up for a short time."

"At mid-day, then," Pereira suggested to Cyrino, in a very low voice, "you send to call the girl and give her the medicine. Do you hear? I have told them already inside there. But I have to keep a sharp eye on the big bicho. He seems like a puma waiting for a wild deer of the plains. I say, don't you think this

---
[27]Inhabitants of the Sertão.

CHAPTER XIII: SUSPICIONS.

wine has some witchcraft in it, eh?"

His companion energetically repudiated such a possibility.

"Well, I don't know that, I am not so sure. These 'inamoratos' are capable of anything. Have you never heard of the love pills and potions, eh? Now tell me have you never?"

"Do not disturb yourself, Senhor Pereira," replied Cyrino, "I will examine the liquid, but I am certain that there is nothing noxious in it."

"Very well then, exactly at mid-day call Maria Conga or Tico. 'Nocencia will somehow drag herself here, and the doctor will give her a dose."

"What! To leave her room already!" observed Cyrino, in a tone of consternation. "No, Senhor, that I will not consent to. I will go and give her the medicine. It will cost me nothing."

Pereira appeared to be perplexed at the suggestion.

"I don't know," he said thoughtfully, but raising his head as an idea seemed to suddenly strike him, he continued: "Very well, I will return here from the plantation, but if I do not appear, then you just step round and make her take a dose. As to this yellow German, I will take him a long way and not bring him back until very late, and he will be so done up with his walk that he will think only of sleeping."

With Pereira occurred a natural, yet comical, fact in the singularities of the moral world. As his suspicions of the intentions of the innocent Meyer increased to exaggerated proportions, he, at the same time, felt an unlimited trust in that other man who was also an absolute stranger, and who at first had caused him to take as many precautions as he was now doing with the other.

Yet withal, in the inevitable struggles of life in which we sometimes find ourselves committed, there is always a certain innate craving for help, a certain desire to meet with some one to aid us, either by strength or counsel, even when a thoughtful reserve or a sympathetic caution prompts us to resist the intervention of those allies of the moment.

Add to this the temperament of Pereira—one predisposed to open-heartedness and garrulity—and then the reason of his doings and sayings in relation to his two guests, Cyrino de Campos and Wilhelm Tembel Meyer, will easily beo comprehended.

CHAPTER XIV: REALITY.

After Cyrino had seen Pereira and his two companions proceed along a stony footpath in the direction of the plantations, and finally disappear behind the orange grove, and as soon as he was thus assured that he was alone, he gave way to the feelings that so strongly agitated him. Sometimes pacing the room with rapid and unquiet strides, sometimes meditating as he lingered with halting steps, at last he went out into the yard, and with uncovered head, and with his hand shading his eyes from the torrid rays of the sun, he stared with a fixed gaze alternately in one or another direction, like one demented.

The day promised to be very warm, for on every side resounded the inevitable indicators of approaching heat, the whirr-whirr and whistle and drone of countless cicadas, while from far away over the plains echoed the noisy clamour of the Seriémas (the snake-eating secretary bird of South America), resembling the noise of a pack of hounds in full cry. Cyrino turned his face to the sun, then, dizzy with the bright glare, and clasping his hands over his dazzled eyes, he returned to the room and recommenced his restless walk.

Why rested not the youth? He had already slung a hammock, and, gently swinging to and fro in the breeze, it seemed to invite him to a comfortable siesta.

Why did he not imitate the proceedings of some little grunters, which, unceremoniously entering the room in search of a cool shade from the fiery sun outside, had found a snug corner, and were now audibly snoring, prisoners of delightful sleep? Outside, the sun shone with resplendent brilliancy, while the shadows of the trees became gradually smaller and smaller. All the animals of the farm prepared for repose. A mare, with her foal, deserted her distant pasture, and sought a shelter from the fierce rays of the sun in the shade of the side of the house, where she remained panting.

To the enervating effect of the summer atmosphere was added the drowsy influence of the monotonous and nasal singing of Cyrino's attendants, who, lazily reclining in the barn close by, accompanied their sleepy refrains on tri-cord guitars.

Meanwhile, the young man resisted all these drowsy influences, and, with increasing restlessness, he continually consulted his watch, taking it from his pocket and returning it at almost every instant. The seconds, the minutes, the hours passed by. Finally, with a deep sigh of relief and satisfaction, he cried:

"Mid-day! Ah, I thought it would never arrive!"

Transformed by animation, he at once went out into the yard and called aloud: "Maria! Oh! Maria Conga!"

No one replied. The dogs only barked. Cyrino, after waiting some time, proceeded to the gate in the fence which separated the grounds of the family quarters from the rest of the farm. Here he again called: "Oh, Maria! Maria! are you asleep, old woman?"

Seeing that his cries elicited no reply, he passed onwards in the direction of the back door of the house, slowly however, as though in fear.

"Oh, Maria! Halloa, Aunty! Ho there! House ahoy!" he clamoured.

Finally appeared, not the old slave, but the dwarf Tico, who, with an imperious movement of his head, seemed to inquire

CHAPTER XIV: REALITY.

the cause of alarm.

"Where is Maria Conga?" Cyrino asked, as he approached.

Tico, with a few but expressive gestures, indicated that the black had gone to the stream to wash linen.

"And is there no one else in the house?"

The dwarf assumed an expression of pride, and indicated that *he* was there, and bestowed an angry glance at the imprudent inquirer.

"Good," replied Cyrino, laughing. "Now, little man, you go inside and say to the Dona that the hour has arrived to take the medicine. I have the wine with me, but I require some coffee to be prepared at once."

Making a sign to the so-called doctor to wait outside, Tico disappeared.

"What? Wait out here in the sun," exclaimed Cyrino, in disgust. "Now that is too bad! What a strange little manikin it is!"

Without further ceremony he pushed open the door and entered the house. Presently he heard footsteps, and Innocencia was then seen approaching. She was wrapped in a large mantle of varied colours; and, pushed back from her brow, her long hair hung in sable masses about her, and, by contrast, increased the pallor of her countenance, which, with the dark circles around her eyes, still denoted great weakness. But when she perceived Cyrino the damask cheeks blushed, like rose-buds impatient to expand into bloom and crying for admiration of their charms.

On reaching the doorway she stopped, and, leaning against the door-post, showed by glances of hesitation that she was undecided what to do.

Cyrino, on seeing her, nervously advanced a few steps towards her, until he in his turn also halted by the side of an old-fashioned high-back chair, an ancient and solid piece of furniture brought by Pereira from his old home in Piumhy. It was with considerable effort that he articulated:

"Then—Donazinha—How are you?—Do you feel better?"

"Better, thank you," responded Innocencia, in a flute-like but very tremulous voice.

"Have you partaken of anything?"

"Yes, Senhor; the wing of a fowl, and with some appetite."

"Do you still feel weak?"

"The weariness is passing away."

Meanwhile, as Cyrino gradually regained his calmness, he slowly approached nearer and nearer to the maiden, an action which seemed to cause her to timidly cling to the friendly door-post as to a shelter. Presently they stood face to face, she on one side of the doorway and he by the other, and both of them were so evidently embarrassed that there was ample reason for the dwarf Tico's look of astonishment, as, bolt upright on his little legs, he stood in front of them. By an effort, Cyrino mastered his emotion, and, outwardly calm in his manner, he continued:

"Well, Dona, the hour has arrived for taking the medicine."

"Already, Senhor Doctor?" implored Innocencia.

"Yes, Dona."

"But I have nothing the matter with me now."

CHAPTER XIV: REALITY.

"You may think so, but it is necessary to entirely eradicate the evil. Suppose it was to return, what a poor doctor you would take me to be."

"The remedy is so unpleasant," she observed.

"It is not nice, truly, but it will give you back your health. With a little courage, you will be able to take it without much trouble. Let me share it with you— —"

"Oh, no!" protested Innocencia.

"It is but to show you, that—that I will do anything for you."

The girl crimsoned with a blush and raised her eyes in surprise, but immediately lowered her gaze as she met the earnest glances of Cyrino.

"The medicine!" she at last suggested, in a low voice.

"Ah! Certainly," exclaimed Cyrino. "Go, Tico, go and fetch coffee from the kitchen, bring also a cup and saucer. Do you not understand?"

The dwarf, however, replied only by a glance of defiance, and moved not.

"Are you deaf?" inquired Cyrino.

"No," responded Innocencia. "Tico sometimes shams like this from wilfulness." In a soft voice and with a tender glance she said to the little man, "Go, Tico, it is for me, do you hear?"

The physiognomy of the dwarf was immediately transformed. A pleasant smile played upon his lips, and he nodded his head two or three times in afiirmative response, but quickly his rugged little brows were knitted into a frown and his eyes moved with restless glances of indecision.

Innocencia had to repeat her request more strongly: "I have

already asked you once, Tico, must I say again, go and fetch the coffee."

At this order he hesitated no more, and slowly went away, glancing backwards several times ere he entered the kitchen, where he delayed but a short time.

Cyrino, in this interval, examined the pulse of Innocencia, who held out her wrist as far as possible. But he, overcoming the weak resistance of the girl; covered with ardent kisses the hand he had secured.

"Meu Deos!" she stammered, "what is this? Look, Tico comes."

The youth immediately stepped back a pace or two, and, in order to cover his confusion, he advanced towards the dwarf, who brought a tin mug in one hand and a cup and spoon in the other.

"That's right," said Cyrino, "put them all on the table."

Rapidly preparing the remedy, he presented it with an unsteady hand to Innocencia, who, without hesitation, drank it at a draught.

Now, whether from the effect of the excitement she had experienced in her state of debility, or whether that was the hour when the ague usually returned, certain it is that she had to suddenly grasp the door-frame to prevent herself from falling.

"Ah! The Dona is fainting," pitifully exclaimed Cyrino.

The dwarf hastened to her assistance, but Cyrino clasped her in his arms and her head reclined upon his breast. His anxiety, mingled with an inexpressible feeling of ecstasy at the situation, created such an emotion within him that his

CHAPTER XIV: REALITY.

laboured breathing soon restored her to consciousness and brought a flush to her pallid face.

"I am better now," she murmured, as she endeavoured to remove herself from the grasp of Cyrino.

"Do not vainly imagine you have recovered," he protested. "Let me lead you to that chair."

With all due tenderness he assisted her to a seat, and removed from her face and shoulders the lonotresses of disarranged hair.

"What a mass of hair it is!" he exclaimed, half smiling.

Tico followed all that action of the scene with marked attention. On seeing Innocencia become unconscious, he raised a strange dumb cry of despair, and afterwards, when he followed her to the chair, he knelt before her and contemplated her with wistful glances of anxiety.

Cyrino endeavoured to utilise the occasion to attempt a reconciliation with the dwarf.

"You are anxious, eh, Tico? It is nothing really. Your mistress will soon be well."

The dwarf, on hearing this exordium, promptly rose to his feet, and replied to the sympathetic announcement of the young man with such a look of contempt and indifference, as thought he would say, "Do not interfere with me; I wish to have nothing to do with you, you doctor of mystery."

"Now," said Cyrino, addressing Innocencia, "you must take a few drops of wine, and you will soon see what strength it will give you."

Uncorking the bottle with the aid of a long pointed knife he carried in his waist-belt, he poured a portion of the wine into a cup and offered it to his patient.

The invalid moistened her lips with a little and thanked the attentive youth with an enchanting smile.

Decidedly that medico pleased her. He had cured her of her physical ailments, and now he attended to her mind. Few men had she hitherto seen, except her father, Manecão, and the old blacks; and, absolutely ignorant of most things and of the ways of the world, well might she think that no man could compare in grace and beauty with the one now before her. Besides, what a mysterious bond of sympathy attached her to that stranger, arrived from she knew not whence, and about to depart, and perhaps never to be seen by her again.

Who knows but that the gentleness and the kindness which Cyrino had showed in his actions towards her were not the only cause of the new sentiment, which, really unknown to her, was as suddenly born in her breast as the flowers of the campos burst into bloom after the rain? A sense of gratitude also added its influence to her feelings.

As these thoughts passed rapidly through the mind of Innocencia, she raised her grand and limpid eyes and gazed at Cyrino with a glance so frank and clear that it seemed to form a broad and open entrance to the inmost recesses of her mind.

"I feel so well now," she said, in her soft, clear, and musical voice, "so light in my body, that it seems impossible I can ever again be miserable."

"No, certainly not," exclaimed Cyrino; "never more. Besides, here am I, and— —"

The commencement of the doubtless would-be pretty speech was interrupted by the arrival of Maria Conga, the old

CHAPTER XIV: REALITY.

negress, returning from the stream with a huge bundle of linen, which she unceremoniously commenced to extend on long horizontal bamboos placed on forked sticks stuck in the earthen floor of the adjoining room.

Cyrino prepared to depart.

"Now," said he, as he took the hand of Innocencia, "keep quiet for a little while. Later on, take some broth, and—ah, Innocencia, do you wish me well?"

"Oh, Maria Santissima! Why should I not wish you well?" she ingenuously inquired. "Mecê[28] never did me any harm."

"I?" ejaculated Cyrino, with energy; "I do you harm? Rather would I die! Yes, Dona, from my soul I——"

Without concluding, he suddenly bade her "Adeus," and departed.

With a slow step he left the room, and when, outside the house, he passed a window close to which Innocencia was seated, he took advantage of the opportunity for a last word.

"Take care," he advised, as he leaned on the window-sill, "take care to avoid the nightdew."

"Nhor-sim" (Sim, Senhor).

"Do not drink any milk."

"So Mecê has already told me."

"Eat only sun-dried meat."

"I know."

"Then adeus—adeus, thou beautiful girl!"

---

[28]Mecê (pronounced Messey) is a provincial corruption of Vossa Mercê, i.e. your Grace, your Worship, a term of civility used by Brazilians to every well-to-do person.

With an effort he tore himself away from where he felt he could remain until old age weakened his limbs.

CHAPTER XV: THE ADVENTURES OF MEYER.

Towards the close of evening, Meyer, José Pinho, and Pereira returned, accompanied by three very old slaves; those from their labours in the field, the former from their entomological excursions.

The Mineiro entered with a merry face, and with boisterous shouts awakened Cyrino, who meanwhile had fallen asleep to dream all the time of his graceful patient.

"Ho! ho! there, my friend! Ho! ho! doctor," shouted Pereira in a resounding voice. "This is what is life, eh? Whilst we are working, I and José's Mochu, you are asleep on a downy couch."

"It is true," assented the young man. "You had hardly gone away when here I laid me down to stretch my limbs, and, until now, I have had one long slumber."

"And the medicine for the girl?" inquired Pereira, lowering his voice.

"Dear me! I really quite forgot, but it will do no harm—that is, if she has no return of fever. Ah! Wait, let me see. yes, now I remember. I gave it to her, of course I did—what was I thinking about?—but I am still half stupid with sleep."

Pereira laughed aloud, and observed, "These doctors kill people as heedlessly as if they were only wild dogs of the forest. In an instant they will forget whether or no they gave medicine to a Christian.'"

Seeing that Meyer had left the room, he suddenly altered his tone, and proceeded to observe very quickly and in a low voice:

"What do you think? Would you believe it? That German has been all day long trying to converse about the girl!"

"Really?"

"It is so—and—and here am I bound by my offer to take him to dinner inside there! Not if I know it, oh no! He may get cross and angry if he likes at my ways, but he does not put a foot again in a room of my family, not if I know it. Heaven deliver me!"

At supper time, Meyer expressed some surprise at again seeing the meal spread in the front room; not that he had any motives for desiring another place, but being so methodical in all his habits, he had fixed in his mind the promise of Pereira, and thought it his duty to remind him of it.

The excuses promptly tendered by the Mineiro had been already thought of, and were, moreover, endorsed by Cyrino, who explained that he had recommended that the patient should be kept perfectly quiet and almost in solitude.

Peirera expressed his acknowledgment in the most openhearted manner. "I see," he whispered to Cyrino as he pressed his hand, "that the doctor is a serious man, one on whom one can depend. Let it be, Manecão will have to be your friend. That—that is certain. Good people deserve to be known and esteemed. But oh! do look at that owl there, eh? What a cunning one! eh? Never mind, he shall pay for it."

If Pereira appeared troubled, the naturalist, on the contrary, was a picture of placid contentment.

"Senhor Doctor," he declared to Cyrino at the supper table, "I

CHAPTER XV: THE ADVENTURES OF MEYER.

am really very contented with my stay here. I have found to-day more curious little bichos than I have met with in all the zones through which I have travelled."

"You cannot imagine," interrupted Pereira, and addressing himself to Cyrino, "what this Senhor does when he is in the woods. He will tumble into some hole and break his blessed neck some of these days, for he tears along with his nose in the air and never looks where he is going. I don't know how it is that he does not get his eyes poked out, for he takes no notice of the branches or anything else; all he wants is to place his hand on the blessed insects. I have already cautioned him several times, now his head, now his hand."

The warnings of the Mineiro proved, indeed, to be judicious and called for, so much so, that, when at this moment Meyer happened to turn round, Cyrino noticed for the first time that his face was cut and very much scratched.

"What is this, Senhor Meyer?" he inquired, in surprise. "Have you been having a tussle with some jaguar?"

"Oh! It is nothing," phlegmatically responded the German.

"And your clothes are all soiled from head to foot with clay."

Pereira burst out laughing.

"There is such a story about this man," said he. "I will just tell you what happened to him. My friend, have you not heard of the saying, 'Trust in the Virgin and don't run, or see the fall you will have!' Oh, it has been *such* a day! Why, I just laughed until I could laugh no more. Only imagine seeing, as I have already told you, this Senhor Meyer tearing and leaping through the woods as though he were a deer of the forest. Now, José Pinho, who has got his head screwed on the right way, he always keeps to a clean path, he does——"

"Lazy fellow," observed Meyer.

"Wise he is though," replied the Mineiro;—but as I was saying, here was the Senhor with his leaps and bounds like a wounded tapir. No sooner did any flying bicho appear, than, zas! away he goes after it, regardless of boughs, branches, thorns, or any coiled up-snake on the ground; but with that net of his he always captured the little bicho. Well, I went off to see after the blacks, and left the man dashing through the bush, while José, in a shady nook, was soon snoring like one possessed.

"I! no Senhor," protested José Pinho.

"Yes, you," corroborated Meyer, with more or less energy. "Lazy fellow! Come, pass the tobacco."

"Very well," continued Pereira, "two or three hours afterwards the Mochu returned in the state you see him in now, and bringing with him a box full of wild bichos."

"Yes, and are they pretty ones?" inquired Cyrino.

"All gone," replied Meyer, in a dolorous tone; "my labour was all lost. I had captured five new species—a fall——"

"Oh! Do let me tell the story," impatiently interrupted Pereira. "Ho! ho! I laughed, oh, how I laughed!" and, to confirm the assertion, he again burst into roars of laughter, in which he was joined by José Pinho and Meyer, "The Mochu seemed very much delighted with the results of his work, and showed me with such pride his box full of beetles and all kinds of bichos, even to cicadas, just as if he had got a king inside it. He had something of everything. Afterwards, when we were returning from the plantation, he saw a red 'insect' perched on a rotten tree trunk, and straightway hurried off to to capture it. I cried out to him, 'Look out, there is a pit there! and the

CHAPTER XV: THE ADVENTURES OF MEYER.

tree is rotten, and you will roll down the precipice so that not even your soul you will save.' Bah! The man is as obstinate as a pack-mule. I shouted to him, 'Take care, Mochu!' But there! He commenced to clamber over a network of vines which covered the mouth of a pit as deep as anything in this world. Just as he was about to place his hand on the said red bicho, he caught hold of the rotten tree, and—zas!—down he went, uttering a screech, like the cry of a cotia. He had just time to clutch at the brambles, and there he hung between life and death, calling out, 'Júque! Júque!' I, when I saw this, sent in all haste to the plantation for a long pole, and if it had not arrived soon, the Senhor Meyer and all his bichos together would have rolled down to the bottom of that abyss——"

"No," replied the German, "the bichos rolled down first, the box open and its contents all go to the bottom."

"All right then. Well, the Mochu clung to that pole tooth and nail, whilst we slowly hauled him up, slowly and fearsome like—eh! so fearful, Maria Santissima!"

After a short pause he continued:

"We have not yet come to the funniest part of it. Ah! you can just prepare yourself for a good lump of laughter. When the Mochu found his feet on solid earth, he commenced to jump about like a crazy goat, to here, to there, he leaped and leaped, again and again, and screeched and squealed as if he was being skinned. He was—ho! ho! ho! ha! ha! ha!—covered with novata ants."[29]

"Yes," exclaimed Meyer savagely, "rotten wood ants, Mein Gott! I jump, I groan, I tear off mine clothes until I was naked as when I was born. Horrible things! Oh, ants of the diabo! They swarmed all over my body, and such pain."

---
[29] The sting of these ants is extremely painful.

Pereira, Cyrino, and José Pinho received with renewed shouts of laughter this violent outburst.

"Perhaps," observed the Mineiro, "this may cure you of your mania of not listening to those who know about these things," and turning to Cyrino: "The truth is, that his body—ah! what a body it is, Senhor Doctor, so white!—became so swollen and blistered that we had to rub him all over with tobacco leaves. Afterwards he took a bath in the stream."

"All would have been well," observed Meyer, "if the box had not opened and dropped all my work to the bottom of the abyss."

"Well, well, we will see to that to-morrow," his servant philosophically observed.

Pereira, recovered from his fit of hilarity, approached close to Cyrino, and observed in a low voice:

"Ah, doctor! Do you know I had half a mind to let that German drop into the pit. If he had not been my guest and recommended by my brother, on my word of honour, I would have given him a shove towards 'inferno,' I would indeed; and you know I am no milk-sop."

"But why?" inquired Cyrino, simulating

CHAPTER XV: THE ADVENTURES OF MEYER.

surprise,

"Yet you ask me why! Because the man did nothing but talk of 'Nocencia all day long. He again told me that she was very beautiful, and a lot of other things—asked if she was married, and, if not, he said it was necessary for the welfare of women to get married, and then I don't know what else. This is an abandoned brute—an 'inamorato.'"

"Nonsense, Senhor Pereira," protested Cyrino.

"I tell you he is. Do you think I am a snake with two heads and cannot see?[30] Ah! What a weight of care is a daughter, and one who is already promised. This is confusion indeed! What my son-in-law Manecão would say to it all, I know not.

"He could say nothing," replied the young man; "and besides, there is no want of those who want your daughter."

"Thank heaven, no, there is not, certainly! But I do not intend that she should be handed from hand to hand. She marries Manecão, or——"

"Or what?" inquired Cyrino uneasily, but simulating indifference.

"Or I will kill any one who tries to tempt her to do otherwise. With me, no one shall play the fool. Ought I not to take a thousand precautions, when I see this yellow-haired foreigner plying his monkey-tricks on the weaknesses of women?"

"Until now he has done nothing,"

"Wah! What would you? Until now he has done nothing but talk of the poor girl, whom may the Senhora Sant'Anna ever protect! I know him now, and may monkeys eat me if ever he

---

[30] The Amphis boena, a common snake allied to the glow-worm, which is popularly supposed to have a head at each extremity, but without eyes.—[Transl.]

sets eyes on 'Nocencia again!" In a still lower voice Pereira continued: "I sounded José Pinho about his master. Said I to him, 'Your patrão is a diabo amongst the women, eh? He is a knowing one, eh?' 'No, Senhor,' he replied at once. I swallowed that lie, and said to him, 'Nonsense, you Carioca have had dust thrown in your eyes.' 'I?' said he; 'not likely.' 'Then have you not seen what your patrão has been doing?' 'He has been a saint,' returned the humbug. 'In Rio?' 'Yes.' 'In the Corte?' 'Yes, in the Corte. But when he was there he went every night to a Beer Garden and chatted and supped with women there, all handsome and well dressed, some with their throats and arms bare——"

"He related all that?" observed Cyrino, doubtfully.

"He did," Pereira affirmed. "See what a man he is! Eh? He is a rascal! This night and henceforward I will sleep in this room and watch if he dares to move from his bed. Ah, if I could only —I would fall on him with a cudgel, so that his ribs would be knocked into little pieces."

The imprudent stories of José Pinho completed the last stone to the edifice of suspicion which the imagination of Pereira had so rapidly raised to the detriment of Meyer. What vestiges of truth really existed in them related only to some hours of leisure during his stay in Rio, which the naturalist passed in the consumption of lager beer in the German café, Cidade de Coblentz, where, at times, he entered into jocular but innocent conversation with certain persons of the feminine sex, frequenters of that establishment, and of manners and customs not perhaps of the most rigorously-moral character.

CHAPTER XVI: THE DYSPEPTIC PATIENT.

According to his intention, Pereira that night brought his hammock to the guests' room with the full resolve of initiating his system of vigilance (although, in any case, it was absolutely useless in relation to the person suspected). Anyhow, he had barely reposed in his easy couch more than a few minutes, before the sonorous sounds of his slumber mingled with those of the heavy breathing of Meyer.

If he had not trusted so much to the watchfulness of his eyes, or rather, if sleep had not, as usual, attacked him so irresistibly, he would naturally, and in a short time, have had his attention attracted by the strange proceedings of Cyrino. For really, the manner in which he passed his nights was alone sufficient to create doubts in the most unsuspecting of minds. Ever restless, he would continually turn on his couch and heave such sighs as only those in dire or imagined tribulations can utter, or he would arise and go out to the yard, to pace to and fro, smoking cigarettes without end, until the cocks on the barn or in the trees hard by announced the first rays of dawn.

It was indeed a lacerating passion that filled the breast of that young man. One of those sudden and irrepressible passions that dominate and overpower the mind, thrilling every nerve as with electricity, and suffocating as the serpents of the Laocoon. Knowing, as he did, all the customs of the Sertão, so rigid in the absolute yoke of prejudice, he foresaw so many difficulties, that if on the one hand they tended to dishearten him, on the other those very difficulties acted as so much fuel to the fire of his newly-born but already overpowering sentiments.

"Heaven help me!" he murmured to himself; "what I only desire is the friendship of Innocencia." It seems ages ago since I saw her. Ah! if I should see her no more, I would put an end to my life." His heart throbbed violently. The blood coursed through his veins with vertiginous rapidity, obscuring his vision and flushing his face with waves of burning heat.

"Nossa Senhora da Abbadia!" he cried, and clutching his hair in his despair. "Save me in this hour of trial! Grant me, at least, hopes that that girl may wish me well—I desire no more. Oh, that this fire that consumes me may find in her heart some responsive warmth!"

This fervent prayer to the Saint of the special devotion of Goyaz served for a while to calm the shattered nerves of the youth, and presently be fell into a fitful slumber, yet only a few instants afterwards to awaken with a sudden start and become still more unnerved.

He was up and moving about when Pereira arose from his hammock. "Halloa!" the latter observed, "you are an early riser to-day."

"Well, it is not my habit," replied Cyrino, "but I have passed these last nights very badly."

"Truly, you do not look up to much."

"I believe the ague has got hold of me."

"Now that is good! Then the doctor went to borrow the ague of bis patient, eh? But, look you, you must pull yourself together, for to-day some invalids will be here for you to 'inziminar.'[31] The news of your arrival has already spread

---

[31] A local corruption of "examinar," to examine.

CHAPTER XVI: THE DYSPEPTIC PATIENT.

abroad, and the gathering of your pilgrims will not be delayed much longer."

"Here I await them."

"Coelho, of course, will be the first to come. Do not hesitate to ask him a tip-top price."

"No, I rather think I shall abandon my idea of attending to this region, and despatch a messenger to stop the arrival of these people."

"Now that only shows that the Senhor is a man of pride and honour, not like a certain person that I know, eh?" On saying these words Pereira glanced at the yet-slumbering Meyer and contemplated him attentively.

The German was really well worthy of observation, independently of any other motive than one of simple curiosity.

Extended on his back, one long arm and one long leg rested on the ground on each side of his narrow bed of trunks, and, owing to the inconvenient position of his head, his chin was tilted above the level of his brows, and his half-opened mouth displayed a row of excellent teeth.

"Can't he snore, eh?" murmured the Mineiro. "Ugh! you rascal—you—you—but no, it is all the same, you won't humbug me."

As the assumptions of Pereira gradually assumed the proportions of fixed ideas, Meyer, in the simplicity of ignorance, inadvertently constantly furnished elements to cause his host to become more and more assured of his convictions. For instance, at breakfast he bethought him of innocently inquiring:

"And your daughter, Senhor Pereira? How is she? Is she better?"

"What is better, Mochu?" inquired the father, ill-humouredly.

"Her health. Is it better?"

"It is better. It is, it is," testily replied Pereira.

"It is quite good. She is about to make a journey."

"A journey? To where? Is it to the town?"

"Man, Mochu!" ejaculated the Mineiro, in great irritation. "You are like an old woman, you want to know everything."

With much vexation and some surprise Meyer received this rude rebuff, yet, as he considered it to be only expressive of annoyance at his apparently unwarrantable curiosity, he duly hastened to apologise with all sincerity, but unfortunately, in terms which aggravated the situation.

"It is indeed true, Senhor Pereira," said he, "ordinary politeness should not have prompted me to say what I did, but excuse me, I pray; but really, your daughter is so interesting that I cannot but think of her always. I have even some presents for——"

"Keep them, then," growled Pereira, but he smothered the reflection his surly words implied in a fit of coughing, and, in order to avoid a continuation of the conversation, he terminated the repast by rising from the table.

"Here comes Coelho, doctor," he exclaimed, on glancing outside. "Sheeh! How yellow he is! It is a long time since I have seen him. Pooh! He looks like a ghost from the other world. He is the one we were talking about. Put the screw on him, doctor, for he is a miserable sort of——" Interrupting

CHAPTER XVI: THE DYSPEPTIC PATIENT.

himself to greet the new arrival, he cried. "Good eyes see you! If it wore not for having a medico in the house, friend Coelho, we might never expect to see you this way, eh? Is it not so?"

"Ah!" dolefully replied the other, with a low moan, "I am always so ill, I have no liking for anything. But where is he? The man?"

"Here he is."

"I have been told that he has worked miracles. He has made quite a name for himself over there by Parnahyba. Do you know?"

"That he had made a name there, no, but that he is a marvellous surgeon I am certain, for in the twinkling of an eye he put on her feet a member of my household."

"Ah! if he could but cure me—I know not how I could thank him."

"Pay him," promptly suggested Pereira, advocating the interests of his guest.

"Yes, how—pay him?" muttered the sick man, with some hesitation.

"In any case, get off your animal."

He, whom the Mineiro called Coelho, entered the front room and made his salutations to Cyrino and Meyer. He was a man already in years, but more aged through infirmities than with the lapse of time. His brow was rugged with wrinkles, his cheeks swollen, the lips were almost colourless, and his eyes were surrounded by puffy rings.

"Which one of the Senhores is the doctor?" he inquired.

"I am," replied Cyrino, assuming an air of importance.

Pereira intervened with some amiability. "Take a seat, Senhor Coelho," said he; "there is no need to hurry. Rest a little, Have you already breakfasted?"

"The little I eat I have already eaten."

"Well, anyhow, just make yourself at home and then talk with the doctor. But tell me, what is there new up in town."

"Nothing that I know of..But really for more than a year I have had no news from there. Things of the world now trouble me no more. Whoever has no health loses the taste for everything. Ah! It is a calamity."

Whilst Coelho lugubriously delivered himself of his complaints, Cyrino turned over the pages of his inseparable Chernoviz, and took from his trunk some dried herbs, which he placed on the table.

"The Senhor," said he, addressing his patient, "is empalamado."[32]

"It is the truth, Senhor Doctor."

"I, who am not a physician," observed Pereira, "would have said so at once."

"Hush-sh, my friend!" impatiently observed Cyrino, in order to impose silence.

"The Senhor," he pompously continued, "has had for many years repeated attacks of fever and ague, followed in due course by loss of appetite. A bloated and swollen appearance of the body succeeded by emaciation. Little by little he continued to lose strength and energy."

"Perfectly right!" murmured Coelho, who followed with

---

[32] Any one suffering from chronic dyspepsia.

CHAPTER XVI: THE DYSPEPTIC PATIENT.

careful attention the march of the diagnosis.

"Now the Senhor cannot eat, or rather has no desire to do so. Is it not so?"

"Exactly, Senhor Doctor," groaned the patient.

"How this man has read in the books, eh?" whispered Pereira to Meyer, in a tone of admiration.

"Afterwards," continued Cyrino, "you were attacked by great, weakness, so much so that, when you walked, you broke out into a profuse perspiration accompanied by a trembling in all your limbs. The spleen is congested, and so is the liver. At night you experience difficulty in breathing, more especially when seated. Sometimes you cough very much, a dry cough, like that of one who is hoarse."

"Just so," exclaimed the sick man, almost with enthusiasm.

"Well," concluded Cyrino, "as I have already told you. you are empalamado."

"And is there no cure?" dolefully inquired Coelho.

"There is, but the remedy is a violent one."

"Well, so long as it makes me well——"

"Many people," replied Cyrino, " have I cured in a worse state than you are in, but, I repeat, the remedy is a violent one."

"I will take anything," declared Coelho; "but for years I have had such a horror of medicine, and from, none of it have I derived any benefit. Well, we shall see——"

At this moment Cyrino altered the tone of his voice, and, glancing towards Pereira, he observed, "The Senhor well knows that this is my livelihood."

The Mineiro applauded, with a nod of his head, this entrance on business.

Not so, however, did Coelho, for he stuttered, "Ah! I am ready, but I am poor, very poor."

Pereira winked his eye with a comical expression of incredulity.

"I must observe that it is my custom to receive payment in two halves," continued Cyrino, and strongly flushing as he added, "If I speak of that subject now so hastily, it is because I need it. Do you not think so, Senhor Meyer?"

"Certainly, certainly," assented the Grerman. "You have every right to it."

"My friend," observed Pereira, "you do not work for the bishop but to gain a living."

"Well, as I said to you," proceeded the young man, addressing Coelho, "the Senhor will pay me at the commencement and at the end of the treatment; thus there can be no mistakes. Will that suit you?"

"What remedy have I?" sighed Coelho. "I will give you—well, up to thirty milreis, or say forty."

"No, Senhor!" retorted Cyrino. "I charge only one price."

"And how much does that amount to?"

"One hundred milreis."[33]

"One hundred milreis!" exclaimed Coelho.

"Fifty down and fifty at the end."

The sick man moaned aloud at the demand, and muttered to

---

[33]Equivalent to, more or less, ten pounds sterling.

CHAPTER XVI: THE DYSPEPTIC PATIENT.

himself like one in sore distress.

"Oh, neighbour!" cried Pereira. "What is that to you? A mere ear of corn to one who owns a barnful."

"Oh! No, no, it is really not so, I assure you," pleadingly replied the other.

"Now, don't tell falsehoods," continued Pereira. "If you had not got the coppers I would have said so to friend Cyrino; but look you, he is one of our family now, and will only cure us for nothing, eh, doctor?"

"Certainly, certainly," declared Cyrino very readily.

"But with you the case is very different. Besides, for what purpose does a surgeon wander about these wilds? Don't you think he wants to make something out of it? Of course he does, and it is only right that he should."

"But fifty—mil—reis!" exclaimed Coelho, in a mournful voice, "and all in one lump."

During- the discussion, Cyrino maintained a dignified silence, devoting his attention to the pages of Chernoviz, and reading one of his many marginal notes therein.

After a long pause and considerable hesitation, Coelho at last heaved a deep sigh of resignation. "Heigho!" said he. "Well, consider the business closed; but, look you, the price of the medicines must be included in the payment, and the visits must be made in my house."

"Certainly," replied Cyrino. "I will go to your fazenda every day. It is not far from here?"

"No, Senhor. By the road it is only two short leagues."

"Good! Now, as soon as you return home, go to bed at once

and take these powders. Take them in two doses, and then keep perfectly quiet for two or three days. You may feel weak from their effects, but afterwards—" Pausing suddenly, for a few moments, he gazed steadily at Coelho, and then observed, "You really want to be cured, eh?"

"Ah! Do I not?"

"And you have confidence in me?"

"Under Deus, only you can save me."

"Then you will unhesitatingly take what I send you?"

"That I will, even if it were red hot iron."

"Now, mark well what you say, I do not like to commence a treatment and then have to stop it."

"Fear not that with me. To linger on as I have lived is not life. I would rather die."

"Then a few days after you have taken the powders, you will have to take a good big dose of the milk of the jaracatiá tree."

"Jaracatiá!" exclaimed the sick man aghast.

"Jaracatiá!" cried Meyer in his turn. "What is jaracatiá?"

"Why that will burn out the inside of the man," observed the Mineiro.

Cyrino, somewhat offended, brusquely replied, "Senhor Pereira, I am no child; I know well what I am saying. This remedy is a secret of mine; true, it is very powerful, and also very dangerous, but it is not the first, nor the second, time that I have cured the 'empalamados' with it. Everything depends on the quantity and the mode of administering the milk, and for that reason I make no mystery of the recipe. Nevertheless, a very little more than is necessary and the patient is in his

CHAPTER XVI: THE DYSPEPTIC PATIENT.

grave."

"Ugh!" exclaimed Pereira, "such a kind of medicine want not I; I would rather be 'empalamado' all my life and risk a better chance of remaining in this world a little longer."

"What is this jaracatiá?" Meyer again asked.

Coelho, with half closed eyes and drooping head, was evidently deep in the meditation of the pros and cons of his case and the prescribed remedy, at last, in a melancholy voice, he observed, "Well, what is to be, is to be. I accept whatever you order me. Whatever you do is well done. How am I to take the jaracatiá?"

"I will tell you later on," replied Cyrino.

"Meanwhile, when you arrive home, look for one of the trees in your neighbourhood, give three gashes in the trunk near its base, and allow the milk to drip. I myself will then select from it what is necessary. I have every confidence that the Senhor will become perfectly sound again, but always bear in mind that in the business of sickness, more than in anything else, no one can say that so and so will happen. Everything is in the hand of God. He it is who makes the sickness disappear from the body, or sends one to the sepulchre. Every good Christian knows that and should conform to the divine will. What a doctor can do is only to assist nature and lend a helping hand to a body which can, and desires to, arise from a bed of sickness."

"Just so, just so!" ejaculated Meyer, who was engaged at the moment in arranging his collections.

"That is also what I understand," said the Mineiro.

"But what is this jaracatiá, Senhor Pereira?" insisted the

German.

Pereira impatiently turned towards him, and almost shouted, "It is a tree, Senhor Meyer, a tree, a huge tree with small leaves, and bears a fruit full of milk, which burns out the life of any one who tastes it. It is a tree, do you hear? A tree! Ugh!"

"Humph! All! I see," placidly replied the German, although not very much enlightened.

During this time Cyrino had taken from his trunk certain medicinal preparations, which be handed to Coelho with careful instructions for their use.

"Do you experience any nausea when you eat?" inquired the youth.

"Much, Senhor Doctor."

"It is always so, but never mind. After taking the milk of jaracatiá, the appetite will return. At first, you must drink only the raw white of eggs well beaten up, afterwards, little by little, you will be able to take more substantial aliment."

"May Heaven only hear you!"

Pereira, who had gone to the door, presently observed:

"Here comes some one else. I can hear the steps of a mounted animal. Without doubt it is some poor fellow shrivelled up with infirmities. Truly, there is no want of sick people in the world. Yet there is so much wickedness about, that it could not well be less than it is." After a short pause he added, in a tone of surprise, "Hi! hi! Meu Deus! Nossa Senhora help us! Do you know who is coming? It is Garcia, who has had the leprosy more than a year, and yet won't believe he has it. Poor fellow! Without doubt he will pay for his mistake. I am really very sorry for these unfortunates—but I say—there—I don't

CHAPTER XVI: THE DYSPEPTIC PATIENT.

want to see them in my house. Come, come, Senhor Doctor, despatch Garcia at once. One does not play with lepers. From such may the Senhora Sant'Anna deliver us. Even to look at them they say is not good." And Pereira, returning to the room, exclaimed hurriedly, "Oh! pray do not let the man dismount, or I shall perhaps have to be rude to him. For the 'Amor de Deus' go outside there at once. See what he wants, and give him all good wishes on our part. Go! go!" he impatiently vociferated, for at that moment a voice was heard inquiring if Senhor Pereira was at home. The latter, seeing that Cyrino did not hasten as he was desired, or fearing that the new arrival might enter the room, hurried to his threshold and frigidly responded tothe greetings of the man called Garcia.

CHAPTER XVII: THE LEPER.

The new arrival, who had already dismounted, made no effort to advance towards the owner of the house. On the contrary, he somewhat retired, and then remained motionless, leaning against his mule with the reins in his hand.

Pereira, from his post of observation, inquired, in no very pleasurable tone, "Well, Senhor Garcia, how goes it?"

"As it has to be," replied the interpolated. "Bad—or rather, as always."

"Rest assured that I feel very sorry for what you say."

"Is the surgeon here?" inquired Garcia.

"He won't be long before he comes out here to see you. In an instant he will be here."

These ungracious words, however, seemed not to disturb the impassiveness of the unfortunate man; he merely observed with an air of melancholy, "I will patiently wait for him."

"I suppose you will return home to-night?" said Pereira.

"I shall. If night overtakes me on the road, I shall halt at the camp of the Perdizes."

"Ah, truly! There is a shelter there. But are you not afraid of the souls from the other world? They say that the old ranch is haunted."

"I?" exclaimed the unfortunate. "I fear only myself. If some poor departed soul wished to pay me a visit, out of very thankfulness I would kiss his fleshless bones. Look you, Senhor Pereira," continued he in a loud and agonised voice, "beware of me, invite me not to enter your house, for I, in

CHAPTER XVII: THE LEPER.

your place, would have to do the same."

"Oh! Senhor Garcia," feebly protested Pereira.

"No. I tell you this from my heart, I do. In my family we have ever had a perfect horror of lepers. The Senhor cannot imagine how intense—and—ah! I am the first. Many years I lived in doubt—to no one I imparted my suspicions. Suddenly, the horrid tell-tale marks appeared on my skin. No longer was it possible to deceive anyone, not even the blind. Ah! meu Deus! what have I not suffered!"

"May He," interrupted Pereira compassionately, "grant that this doctor may have some remedy. You know sometimes — —"

"What? To cure leprosy?" replied Garcia, with a pungent smile of incredulity. "No! There is not one of the miserable spotted ones who dares even to hope it."

"Then wherefore do you wish to see the medico?" inquired the Mineiro.

"For one thing only. To learn from him from the books he has studied and his knowledge of infirmities, whether this disease is catching. That only is what I desire. For if it is, then will I fly from my home, disappear from this land, and wander far away to some distant corner secluded from the sight of man. But there, some say it is catching, others that is not, that it is a disease of the blood only—I know not."

Upon his rough country saddle he folded his arms, and on them he sadly reclined his head, his face expressive of profound sorrow and despair. After a pause, he raised his eyes to heaven, and exclaimed, "Ah! Deus, Nosso Senhor! what Thou hast ordained, so shall Thy will be done." Then addressing Pereira, he continued, "I would save my family from these—these—marks, and if the medico destroys my feeble hopes, then will I go to S. Paulo."

Pereira cut short this dolorous dialogue. "Very well, Senhor Garcia," said he, "I will send the man to you."

Re-entering the house, he repeated the request to Cyrino, who was then engaged in giving directions to Coelho to take, one month after the jaracatiá, some infusion of certain indigenous herbs, common in the locality.

"Go, doctor," advised Pereira, "go outside there, and see the other poor fellow, and despatch him as soon as possible, for I am getting quite nervous whilst he remains on my lands."

Cyrino then went out, and advancing slowly, he stopped at some paces from the unhappy Garcia, whose countenance thereupon suddenly contracted with an expression of fear and humility, for the action served to confirm his worst fears.

Evening was drawing nigh, and the golden rays of the setting sun gleamed over the stilled landscape with a light so soft and melancholy, that it added to the sadness of the scene, and Cyrino felt his heart oppressed with an involuntary feeling of pity.

The leper gazed at him with glances of keen anxiety and even of awe; for from the lips of the man before him was about to fall his sentence of eternal proscription—a sentence without appeal, irremediable, fatal! Oh! What agony was seen in that gaze! What bitter thoughts! What despair! With eager half-opened mouth he waited for the words of Cyrino to break that cruel suspense.

"Well," said Cyrino, after a short pause, "what is it that the Senhor desires?"

CHAPTER XVII: THE LEPER.

"Doctor," stammered Garcia, "I—first—that is, I want to pay you something—I—I have brought some money, but perhaps it may not be sufficient."

Cyrino interrupted him. "I never accept anything," said he, "for treating the—your complaint."

"That is to say," replied Garcia bitterly, "there is no cure for it. Ah! well I know it, yet it is cruel to ever hear it repeated. Look you, my complaint I have not had long—it is quite in its commencement—who knows—if—if the Senhor does not know of some herbs?"

"Unhappily," responded Cyrino, "neither I, nor any one else know of such plants."

"Well!" said Garcia, with a deep sigh, and closing his eyes as if to concentrate his thoughts, he continued: "Ah! doctor, I am but a poor man, already old and worn out. Why comes not death in place of this corruption that destroys my flesh as if already in the tomb. A long time I have felt it in me, but I kept my secret, I bid it from all, I hid it even to the day on which my granddaughter—the child of my heart—my darling Jacintha—when she, for the first time, feared to embrace me. Ah! Senhor, how I suffer! Ah!" His words seemed to choke him. He turned to a death-like pallor. He gasped, "Ah! water! water!—give me—water, for the love of God! Ah! would that now—my—my hour had come. Ha! my throat I—It burns as a fire!"

Reeling as if in some paroxysm, he fiercely clutched his saddle to save himself from falling, whilst Cyrino ran hastily to fetch water.

"Now, what shall I give you the water in?" inquired Pereira, in reply to Cyrino's demand.

"What you please," replied the young man hastily; "but—see you not how that poor Christian suffers?"

"There, take that earthenware cup. We will break it afterwards," replied Pereira.

The leper eagerly seized the cup and drank the water greedily, after which he seemed relieved.

"It was but a fit of faintness," said he, gradually resuming his calmness. "But as I have already related, long ago I knew I had the 'mal;' now, I only want to know one thing', and then I will leave you. That is—is—is this 'mal' catching?"

"It is," replied Cyrino sorrowfully.

"What is there that I can do?"

"Ask Our Lady Saint Anne for patience and Our Lord Jesus Christ to protect you in your unhappy life!"

Garcia humbly uncovered his head at the mention of the Holy names, and in a low voice he murmured, "Oh! my God, my God! grant me strength—give me courage—to do my duty to Thee. Then, as if taking upon himself some great resolve, he exclaimed, "The will of the Almighty be obeyed. Doctor, I thank you. The poor leper will have to ask the Lord that he will recompense in this world and in the other the man of letters. Adieu! I go to the lands of S. Paulo, where I shall meet with those equally afflicted. Adieu!" Mounting his horse with considerable effort, he turned to the persons who, at a distance, had attended the consultation. "Adieu!" he cried, as he waved his hat. "Friends and countrymen, Senhor Pereira, Senhor Coelho and you all, once more, Adieu! I go to bury myself far away beyond the Parnahyba. This Sertão will never see me again!"

CHAPTER XVII: THE LEPER.

The last words of the unfortunate creature were received in silence."

Clapping spurs to his horse, Garcia departed in the direction of the main road, already darkening as night spread its lugubrious mantle over the leper's dreary way to life-long misery.

CHAPTER XVIII: BITTERS AND SWEETS.

One after the other the days passed by without novelty — Cyrino, diagnosing and curing, or rather prescribing; Meyer in continually adding to his already fine entomological collection, but ever accompanied by Pereira, who cautiously endeavoured to always keep within sight of his guest.

Cyrino, as before, was still the confidant of all the fears of Pereira.

"The German," said the Mineiro, "will not let me rest in peace, yet I so keep him under my eye, that that at least is some satisfaction; but if he gets any suspicions of it I shall get frightened even of my shadow. I am on a fire. I know not why Manecão Doca does not arrive. I do so want to place on the ground this cargo of care. Now, more than ever, 'Nocencia ought to get married. Bah! How these women do worry a man's life out! Ugh! And even all this is nothing to what some of 'em will do."

"Then do you expect Manecão to arrive very soon?" asked Cyrino, changing colour.

"He cannot delay long — in two or three days at the most. He is coming from Uberaba, and, without doubt, he has there arranged all the papers. I gave him the certificates of my marriage and the baptism of the little one — and also advanced him money for the expenses, although he wanted to refuse it."

"Then all is now absolutely decided?" again anxiously inquired Cyrino.

"No doubt of it. Have I not already told you so more than

CHAPTER XVIII: BITTERS AND SWEETS.

once. Now it is only 'a case of bricks and mortar.' I even already treat Manecão as a son, and the honour of this house is also his honour."

"But your daughter?"

"What about her?"

"Does she care for him?"

"Now what next!" exclaimed Pereira with a superb smile of disdain at the question. "A fine fellow like him, and so straightforward! Bah! But even if she does not care for him, it is my will, and there's an end of it. As to her happiness, and as to her being a good daughter, I have no reason to complain; and I am positively sure that the bridegroom will soon wake an echo in her heart. Would that I could now see him arrive."

In the meanwhile the health of Innocencia had been completely restored, and, during the progress to convalescence, Cyrino had seized every opportunity for a. pretext to render her every possible attention. But now, with the rosy flush of health tinging the damask face of the Sertaneja, a reason to visit her no longer existed, and the brief and serious interviews of the medico were terminated by Pereira in order that his attention might not be diverted from the person of Meyer.

Then the young man, with a pang in his heart, declared that his services and his presence were no longer necessary.

Entire weeks now passed away without the young man being once able to catch a glimpse of his loved one; and, with this suspense, his passion became so all-consuming, that, in order to disguise the cause of his nervous irritation, want of appetite, and constant pallor, he again alleged, as the reason of his apparent ill health, a return of an attack of intermittent fever.

The uncertainty in which he lived as to whether his affection was returned or otherwise, gave him accesses of real agony of mind, which, especially in the silent hours of night, tormented him to the utmost limits of human endurance. One night the torment of the young- man acquired such proportions that he resolved, that, on the next day, he would fly from such a place of uncertainty and suffering. Having taken this resolution he felt calmer, and, impressed by the peaceful serenity of the night, he commenced to ponder with more tranquillity on the aspects of his case.

It was then perhaps an hour before the break of day, when the surroundings were only dimly illumined by the shadowed light of a clouded moon, a light, soft, serene, equably diffused throughout the atmosphere, and uninterrupted by any intermittent gleams of moonlight. The cocks had already crowed, and from far away were now and then heard the strange cries of the anhumas-pocas.

Cyrino, as if seized by some new resolve, suddenly rose to his feet. After some hesitation, he passed through the gate of the fence by the side of the house and bent his steps in the direction of the thickly-foliaged orange-grove, amidst the dense shadows of which he watched and waited awhile.

Presently he approached the fence at the rear of the house, from whence, with a beating heart, he perceived, at an open window, a female figure—her figure—Innocencia herself. There could be no doubt of it. For some time she made no movement, but at length she slowly withdrew, and little by little softly closed the window shutter.

Cyrino immediately sprang forward and gave three gentle taps on the shutter.

CHAPTER XVIII: BITTERS AND SWEETS.

"Innocencia! Innocencia!" he called in a low but ardent voice full of supplication.

No one responded.

"Innocencia!" again implored the young man. "Hear me! Open! Have pity on me! I die for your sake."

After a short time, which appeared a century to Cyrino, he tried the window, and finding it unsecured, with great trembling he pushed it open. The girl quickly returned, seeming astonished to behold him there, and frightened to see the shutter apparently open by itself.

Wishing to give some, or any, pretext for the situation, and simulating surprise, she very softly and stammeringly inquired:

"Why comes—Mecê—here? For what purpose? I—I am well now."

Cyrino reached forward and seized her hands.

"Oh!" cried he passionately. "Ill am I now. It is I who am now about to die, for you have bewitched me, and no remedy can I find for my sickness."

"I? No!" protested Innocencia.

"Yes! You. A girl such as I have never seen. Your eyes burn me. I feel a fire within me. I eat not—I live not. My only desire is to see you—and—and to love you. Sleep! I know no more; and this week I have aged more than I ought to in many years. And why all this, Innocencia? Ah! well you know."

"No, indeed I do not," the girl replied in all sincerity.

"Because I love you.'"

"Wah!" she exclaimed. "Is love, then, suffering?"

"Love is suffering when one knows not if the passion is returned—when he sees not she whom he worships. But when one is as I am now, ah! then, indeed, love is heaven."

"And when you are away?" she inquired. "What is it that you feel?"

"Here, within my breast, by day and by night, there seems to burn a never-ending fire, and I feel as though about to die. All things are hateful. I think only of her my soul craves for; her memory haunts me, in every hour of the day and of the night, in my slumbers, and amid my prayers to Our Lady, she is ever present—she, the well-beloved, and——"

"Oh!" interrupted the girl, with all ingenuousness, "then I also love."

"You?" cried Cyrino passionately.

"If it is as—as Mecê says."

"I—I swear to you!"

"Then—then I love also," declared Innocencia.

"But whom? Tell me quickly. Whom?"

After a pause, and with some hesitation, she replied with some emotion, "Him who loves me!"

"Ah!" exclaimed the young man rapturously, "then you are mine—mine assuredly, for no one in this world—no one, do you hear—is capable of loving you as I do. Not even your father, nor your mother were she alive. Let your heart speak, but if you wish to send me out of this world, tell me that it is not I. Tell me!"

"And how would Mecê die?" she tremulously inquired.

"There is no want of trees to hang me nor water to drown

CHAPTER XVIII: BITTERS AND SWEETS.

me."

"Heaven help me! Don't talk like that. Yet why does Mecê like me so much? Mecê is no relation of mine; not even a distant cousin; he is really even unknown to me. I have seen you but a very short time, and yet—yet you think so much of me."

"And you? Do you not think of me the same?"

"Yes, you. Why are you awake at this hour? It is because sleep deserts you. Because your couch seems, as mine, like a bed of torments. Why do you think of some one at every instant? Yet that some one is not your cousin, not even a distant one, and verily even unknown to you?"

"It is true," Innocencia candidly confessed. "But who told Mecê that I think of him?"

"Innocencia," entreated the young man, "I will not deny it, I knew that I was loved.'"

"Always this thing, love!" she observed, more to herself then to the listener. "Last year, on the occasion of the Festival of Sant'Anna, some people, relatives of mine, came here, and laughed at me because I did not understand them; so much so, that one of them, the Nha Tuca,[34] said to me, 'Really, are you not yet in love with some young man?' I replied that I knew not what she meant. That was absolutely true and as certain as Our Father is in Paradise. Now——"

"And now?"

"Now?" she repeated. "Ah! Who knows if it were not better as it was, and that I had never liked any one?"

"That is not natural. It is against the laws of Heaven. Whatever is destined, must be fulfilled."

---
[34]The Senhora Tuca.

Innocencia yet remained at some distance from the window, so that Cyrino, in order that his whispers might reach her, leant over the window sill and inclined his body towards her. He still retained her hands in his, and tenderly pressed them whenever she tried to withdraw them.

The conversation of the lovers was interrupted by frequent pauses, during which, in the intoxication of their love, they gazed upon each other with dreamy glances filled with passion.

"Ah! Innocencia," cried Cyrino, "let me feast on your face. To me it is more beautiful than the moon; more brilliant than the sun." And in spite of resistance, which although weak he was conscious of, he succeeded in inducing her to approach close to the window sill.

"To love," she observed, "must really be something wrong."

"Why?"

"Because here am I, and my face feels on fire, and a something within me tells me that I am committing a sin."

"You! So pure!" contested Cyrino.

"If some one came here now and saw us, I should die of very shame. Senhor Cyrino, leave me—go away! Your eyes fascinate me. You have bewitched me. That medicine you gave me had some herb in it for me to take, and become—become——"

"No, no," the youth energetically interrupted. "I swear to you—by my mother's soul I do—that the remedy had nothing of the kind in it, absolutely nothing."

"Then why am I thus? I know myself no more. If my father appeared, would he not be right to kill me?"

CHAPTER XVIII: BITTERS AND SWEETS.

Her voice, as she uttered these words, sounded lower and lower, and finally ended in a flood of tears.

Cyrino threw himself upon his knees before her.

"Innocencia," he exclaimed. "By the salvation of my soul, I give you my oath that I have done nothing wrong to win your heart. If you love me, it is because God has so ordained it. I am no man of dissipated habits, and until now I have never loved any woman but you, but how could I help loving a woman such as you are. Oh! pardon me, Innocencia. If you suffer, I also suffer much. Pardon me." Cyrino somewhat raised his voice as he concluded this appeal.

Suddenly Innocencia appeared startled, and trembled as with some fear. "Did you hear that noise?" she asked, in a terrified voice.

"No," responded Cyrino.

"Some one is awake there indoors."

"Well, go and see who it is. If it is nothing, return. I will await here, hidden in the shadow of the wall."

Some moments afterwards the girl returned. "I can see no one," she said.

"Then it was a delusion."

"Oh! Cyrino. You had now better go away."

"No, Innocencia, have pity on me; I shall soon not be able to see you again, and we must converse about arranging our future. The Manecão will not delay."

"Ah!" she exclaimed in surprise; "then Mecê knows."

"I do know; and unfortunately he will soon be here."

"Ah!" she cried. "Well knew I that you would be my destruction. Before seeing you I should have married that man even with joy. It was such a novelty; for he told me he would take me up to town. But now, the idea fills me with horror. Oh! why did you come to disturb my peace. I am only a poor girl who has known no mother since childhood. Are there no other girls in the cities, or in all the wide world? Why did you come to make my heart ache that was so at peace? Why did you come to destroy my sleep? To take away the desire to live as before? So innocently, that, until now, I have never had a wicked thought nor ever done harm to any one."

"And I?" replied Cyrino, with energy. "Think you that I am happy? Mark well one thing', Innocencia, that so sure as God now hears me, you will marry me or I will end my life. What but my ill-luck was the cause of all this misery. If I had only chanced to come here before the arrival of that man—who is now so odious to me that I could slay him—what could then prevent my now being the happiest man in the world? Happier in this wild Sertão than the Emperor in his palace, or the millionaires of Rio de Janeiro. As I have already said, the fault was not of mine, I am not to blame."

"Are there no means to save us?" suggested the young woman.

"Means? I will— —"

At this moment there arose, from the direction of the orange-grove, the sound of a whistle, high-pitched and prolonged, and a stone, impelled by some mysterious hand, came whizzing through the air, and, with great force, struck the wall of the house close to the head of Cyrino.

Innocencia, uttering a half-smothered cry of terror, quickly closed the window shutter, whilst Cyrino dashed towards the

CHAPTER XVIII: BITTERS AND SWEETS.

dark shadows of the grove, in the direction from whence the stone had come.

Despite his eager search he failed to discover a sign or trace of any one, whilst all around still prevailed the calm peacefulness of the night. He searched the recesses of the grove with all his senses, yet heard he only the noise of his own footsteps.

Tired at last, he left the grounds and cautiously wended his way to the front yard of the house. On arriving there he stopped and listened attentively, when again penetrated his ears the sound of the same whistle, but the notes were more strident, more prolonged, and higher pitched.

CHAPTER XIX: HOPES AND FEARS.

During the days of his stay on the lands of Pereira—lands which, except at leagues distant, had neither limits nor neighbours—Meyer increased his interesting collection with an extraordinary variety of "bichos," especially of butterflies.

The pleasure which he experienced in obtaining such a satisfactory result of his labours was so great, that on every occasion he expressed it most heartily—a fact that should have been, of itself alone, sufficient to convince the most incredulous of men as to the question of his sincerity.

"Senhor Pereira," said the naturalist, "I assure you that in no part of Brazil have I yet done so well as on your fazenda."

"I understand you, you rascal," growled the Mineiro to himself.

"Really it is so. The only thing that I regret is that Your daughter is no longer visible. I regret it much, I do indeed."

Pereira forced a sickly smile, and, although clenching his fists and becoming jaundiced with an access of rage, he nevertheless calmly replied:

"Mochu knows this is the custom of my country. Women are not made for——"

"For what?" inquired Meyer, noticing the pause.

"To *prosearem* with anybody."

"What is *prosearem*?"

"Oh! To converse. To let their tongues rattle," hastily

CHAPTER XIX: HOPES AND FEARS.

explained Cyrino.

"Ah! Thank you, doctor," returned Meyer, gratefully acknowledging that philological indication, which was immediately entered in his notebook, as "*Prosearem* is to converse."

"Very good! But truly it is a pity, Senhor Pereira, because your daughter is such a pretty girl."

"Humph! That bait won't take," murmured the Mineiro, "I see I must never take my eyes off this 'bicho.'"

"It is a pity," Meyer repeated two or three times. "A very great pity indeed."

Certainly this language was not likely to vanquish the suspicions of Pereira; in fact his vigilance hourly became, if possible, more keen; but, being concentrated entirely on one person, it afforded all the more liberty to the actual culprit to return and visit the ill-guarded treasure. Yet even so, the desired interview was compassed with difficulty, for the girl had been so impressed with the termination of -the last interview, that for some days she had scarcely left her room.

To write to her was, above all, useless, for the simple reason that she had never learnt to read, and besides, what means existed to send her a note or even a sign? Reasons, therefore, were there in abundance to make Cyrino weary with impatience and nearly desperate with anxiety.

Meanwhile, in the open air and amidst the shadowed seclusion of the orangery, he passed his nights, thinking of how to solve his difficulties, and searching for an acceptable explanation of those two mysterious whistles, and, above all, of that vigorously-thrown stone—one so well directed, that, but for a little deviation of aim, it might have stretched him upon the ground.

On one of these watchful nights of anxiety, he had the satisfaction to see, at last, Innocencia's window reopen.

The poor girl—consumed with the tumult of her love—had sought relief in an endeavour to inhale with the fresh dew-laden gentle breeze of the Sertão night somewhat of its tranquillity, so that its peaceful influence might serve to calm the violence of the sensations that so strongly agitated her. and—who knows?—possibly to see, if by chance he might be there, the one who had created so much disturbance in her breast.

Rapid as the flight of an arrow, rapid as that savagely-thrown stone, Cyrino flew towards the opening window, and covered with ardent kisses the hands of his beloved.

"The cry?" she at once anxiously inquired. "The two cries? And the stone? What of them?"

"Oh! It was nothing," Cyrino hastily replied. It was only a macanan;[35] and what you thought was a stone was but a noitibo[36] that flew by me and struck against the moonlit wall."

"Really?" she incredulously inquired.

"Really. I also, at first, was very much alarmed. Afterwards I verified that it was nothing but a delusion. At night one sees marvels in everything. But to me, the only one I see is yourself. My life! My angel of heaven!"

With this madrigal, Cyrino opened a conversation similar to that of the first night. One such as two ardent lovers lisp and coo in the eternal, yet ever new, declaration of love, such as

---

[35] A species of hawk.

[36] A night bird.

CHAPTER XIX: HOPES AND FEARS.

has been repeated over and over again since the days when Adam and Eve first practised it under the shade of the divine trees of Eden.

The young man expressed some fears that the presence of Meyer might produce a possible rival. She laughed merrily at the suggestion, and jested with spirit, yet kindly, at the queer figure of the foreigner. Presently they began to discuss their prospects and lay out the plans of a happy future life.

"Now that I know what love is, I will plainly tell my father that I cannot marry Manecão," said Innocencia.

"But suppose he objects?"

"Then will I cry—cry bitterly."

"Tears will serve no end."

"But I have yet another resource."

"What is it?" inquired Cyrino.

"To die!"

"No! Oh! say not that. There are yet other means. I will tell you— —"

Innocencia, with a grave air, interrupted him.

"Listen, Cyrino," she said. "During these days I have learnt many things. Before this I went through the world as though I were blind and knew nothing wrong in it, but the passion that I have for Mecê is as a sudden flash of light within me, for now I begin to see better. No one has said anything to me, but it seems as if my soul has awakened to counsel me as to what is good and what is evil. I know that I ought to fear you as one who can destroy me; I know not how it is, yet I feel that my honour and that of my family are all in your hands— —"

"Innocencia!" Cyrino interrupted.

"Let me speak. Let me explain to you what fills my breast, and then I shall feel at peace. I am a child of the Sertão; I have never read books, neither have I had anyone to teach me anything; if I vex you, pardon me, for I do it unwittingly. I remember a long time ago when some men and women stopped here I asked my father why he did not invite them inside the house, as you know is customary with families. My father answered, 'No, 'Nocencia. These are abandoned women of gay lives.' I was very much astonished. 'All the better then,' said I, 'if they are gay and merry they ought to divert me.' 'They are abandoned people and have no shame,' continued my father. I felt so sorry for them you cannot imagine. Afterwards, I went to take a peep at them. Hi! What bad ugly words they used! How they scolded and quarrelled, and smoked and sang aloud, and drank aguadente until they reeled and fell to the ground. And it was men who made the poor things like that! Ah! Better to die. It seems to me that Nossa Senhora ought to take pity on those who love, but certainly to forsake those who go wrong. If there is no other remedy, let us at least remember that our souls, when they have finished with this world, will fly to the starry heavens to there wander as in a garden. Were I to die and Mecê also, my soul would fly through the air searching for Mecê, searching, ever searching, until found, and then together we could fly to here, to there, sometimes by the road of S. Thiago,[37] sometimes descending to this Sertão to see where they have laid our two bodies. Ah! That would be delightful!"

Innocencia thus showed that she possessed an exalted imagination and a pure and elevated mind. Enveloped in her purity, as in a mantle of bronze, she freely and naturally

---

[37] The milky way, so designated in Portuguese.

CHAPTER XIX: HOPES AND FEARS.

expressed her new feelings and sentiments without reserve. Yet this modest and delicate nature, in a way, so impressed Cyrino, that an invincible diffidence held him a captive before the weak young girl, who, of the mysteries of existence, only knew that she loved.

Thus it was, therefore, that he no longer allowed the thought to pass through his mind of leaping through the window, nor of dwelling upon thoughts even less decorous. He consumed the time in bathing with kisses the hands of his inamorata, in the endless chatter of lovers, in protests, in vows, and in forming sweet dreams of the future.

"To-morrow," said Cyrino, "I will cautiously approach your father, get him to talk about your marriage, and then lead the conversation round to myself."

"My father," observed the girl, "is very good, but I am in such fear of him. Ah, meu Deus! He has such a temper."

"I have great hopes, nevertheless," replied Cyrino. "I shall be very explicit and speak plainly. What I desire is that you may be constant to me."

The vague sense of dread that held possession of Innocencia was also fully shared by Cyrino, so much so, that when day arrived his courage failed, and he ventured not to broach the question to Pereira, although the latter's continued complaints against Meyer permitted ample opportunities to enter upon the subject, and, had Cyrino been so disposed, he would have been easily enabled to furnish a theme for the decisive conversation he desired to open.

Yet although the succeeding days passed away one after another without bringing any modification of the state of affairs, sweet hopes yet lingered in the heart of Cyrino—

dreams, picturing a happy life to come and a happy issue from the tangled thread of doubt and tribulation in which he lived.

CHAPTER XX: FRESH ANECDOTES OF MEYER.

One day, Pereira, on returning from his daily labours, showed another phase of his now habitual irritation against Meyer. Downcast and sullen in expression, he made signs to Cyrino that he desired to speak with him alone, and both men, without uttering a word, walked on until they reached the borders of a stream about a mile from the house.

"What is the matter with the man to-day?" Cyrino said to himself. "Perhaps the moment for treating of that business is about to arrive. Who knows?"

On reaching the banks of the stream, Pereira suddenly faced his companion, and, in an altered voice loud and harsh, he delivered himself of a series of exclamations.

"Know you, Senhor Doctor, that I can stand this German no longer? He is a vagabond! He is a puma fresh from inferno come to utterly destroy me! My brother! Ah! My brother, what a present you have sent me!"

"But what has happened now?" inquired Cyrino.

"Look you, if it were not for that letter and the word I gave to the cursed villain—a hundred lightnings blast him! Anaconda of the diabo! The ginger colt!—a ball would ere this have already scattered his brains."

"Senhor Pereira, what has he now done?" again inquired Cyrino.

"I came here just to relieve myself of this load on my heart — —"

"But— —"

"You know that Mochu is worse than a black jaguar, although he appears like a man who would not harm a flea, yet that man is truly a damned soul—a seducer— —"

"Always these suspicions!" observed Cyrino.

"Suspicions? No, they are certainties. Why, what does the man talk about all day long? Is he not always thinking of the girl? He opens any conversation with the eternal question. How is your daughter? 'She is well,' I tell him, once and for all, yet still he insists all the time in talking about her. It makes my blood boil, and still I try to speak him fairly. To-day he came out of his disguise, and said to me as calmly as though he were lapping bread and milk, 'Your daughter is about to marry?' 'She is,' I replied as savagely as I could. 'And with whom?' I had half a mind to say to him, it is no business of yours, you intriguer, and then to crack his head with a cudgel, but as he is my guest I quietly replied, 'With a man of the Sertão, who would grind his knife into the bowels of whoever would interfere with bis wife.' The German pretended not to understand me, and with the greatest impudence be retorted, 'The Senhor does wrong. Your daughter is so wonderfully beautiful that she ought to marry some one from the cities.' At this I lost my patience. 'Mochu,' said I to him, 'every one orders his own household as be thinks best, and here I do not want to be interfered with.' He, when he saw me black with rage, begged me to excuse him, and recounted a long rigmarole about this, that, and the other, and as to what was good for my daughter, and I know not what besides, all in a gibberish sort of language that I little understood."

"He certainly did wrong," observed Cyrino.

"Is there any question of it? Ah! that is a body that ought to be

CHAPTER XX: FRESH ANECDOTES OF MEYER.

soused into the sugar boilers of Pedro Botelho. He is a Jew, and, above all, a hunter of 'inesects,' and saying that I have said everything. But stay, I have not told you the rest. To-day it really seems as if he was possessed of the devil. Close to where I was working in the plantation with my captives,[38] he entered the adjoining woods, and there he made such a row in breaking through the branches and vines that one would have thought a tapir was charging there. Suddenly I heard a great uproar and shouting; it was Meyer and his man José Pinho bellowing like two minhocões.[39] I ran to see what it was, and found them very contentedly gazing upon a bicho they had pinned to a stick. 'Halloa!' said I, 'what is all this?' The German commenced to jump about like a young goat. 'It is new!' he cried to me. 'It is new!' 'What is new, Mochu?' 'This bicho,' said he. 'For no one has discovered it before me. It is my own, do you understand, my own discovery? And I am going to give it the name of your daughter.' Now, just think of that. Why, when I heard it I was so beside myself with rage that my mouth became so parched that I could not swallow the saliva. Just think of it! The name of 'Nocencia amongst a lot of bichos! It seems even a mockery, a derision. Now I want the doctor to tell me what I ought to do, or at least try to help me. I cannot send a ball into that rascal as he deserves, yet it is too much to have him in the house. It is really too much. I ask your counsel. Fortunately I have taken care to keep him away from the house, and the girl has no suspicion of anything. On the other hand, woman as she is, she will yet give me enough to do. And then again, I cannot imagine why Manecão does not arrive. He is the only one who can free me from this

---

[38] Slaves.

[39] Minhocões are mythical animals of the Sertão, which are said to bellow with a great noise. It is likely that they are monstrous anacondas or water boas, that are known to make such noises when disturbed.

torment. Once that that German sees the girl with her husband I shall then feel at ease. Don't you think so? Look you, on my word of honour, to be thus is not life. I was made to say what I think, and treat everybody well, but these moods that I have now, God only knows what they cost me. Even my work suffers, for my foreman is a good-for-nothing old black, and, instead of looking after the negroes, very often I have to leave the plantation and trot after those blessed bichos, so that that Jew shall not leave my sight. Ah! My brother, what a load you have put ou my shoulders! I, however, was not born to hide what I feel within me," and Pereira, with his heart filled with his tribulations, threw himself with desperation, rather than seated himself, upon a mound of earth close by.

Cyrino, with an air of pensiveness, remained standing in front of him, and finally, after a brief moment of doubt, he decided to try his fortune and broach the grave question which meant to him so much happiness.

"Senhor Pereira," said he, in a somewhat tremulous voice, "I think the German does wrong to chatter so much about a person of your family, and he has, indeed, furnished ample reasons for your uneasiness of mind."

"Ah! Doctor, you are indeed a man worthy of all confidence."

"But," continued the young man, with an effort, and pausing at every word, "I think on one point he had some reason. It was when—when he gave you—counsel—that—that the Senhor should not oblige your daughter to marry—like—well, thus—as you purpose—without consulting her wishes—if—if —well there, I don't know—but perhaps the—the Manecão may not please her— —"

Pereira in one bound sprang to his feet, and brought his face, suddenly inflamed with passion, close to Cyrino's.

CHAPTER XX: FRESH ANECDOTES OF MEYER.

"What!" he exclaimed, in a voice of thunder. "What! I—I consult my daughter? Ask her permission to marry her? The Senhor is crazy or else mocking me. Ah!—What! Is it possible, you also——"

A gleam of some vague suspicion flashed from his flaming eyes. Cyrino immediately perceived the delicacy of the situation, and at once proceeded to counteract the bad impression he had evidently created.

"Ha! ha!" said he, with a simulated smile, "It is true. I was quite thinking of the customs of the cities. Here in the Sertão you Sertanejos have very different ideas. Pardon me, Senhor Pereira, but really it is this Meyer who so confounds my thoughts. Well, I believe—now that you have asked my opinion—that the Senhor should continue to keep an eye on the German, and I will endeavour to help you, so far as lies in my power."

Pereira little by little recovered his tranquillity.

"Now," said he, after a short pause, "this state of things cannot last much longer. More than a month that bicho has stopped here, and he has already told me that he will very soon proceed on his journey to Camapuan—but that is only his humbug. He never intends to go there. Still, it is all the same things for one of these days he will get a shot from hereabouts that will drive some sense into his head, or a knife will inquire what he is made of. He won't always be able to have letters from one's brother to get him free from his mischief. May the diabo take him far away! Well! Let us return, Senhor Cyrino; already too long we have allowed the bicho to remain alone."

Both men then returned towards the farm. Cyrino, in the meanwhile, feeling thoroughly disheartened; for the tone of the conversation had utterly destroyed such hopes as had previously animated him of the chance of a happy issue to an endeavour to oppose the projected marriage of his lover with the fatal Manecão. Especially did he feel depressed when, half way home, Pereira abruptly turned to him and peremptorily observed:

"Truly, Senhor Cyrino, those words of yours so stirred up all my blood that I can yet feel it coursing in a gallop through my veins."

CHAPTER XXI: THE PAPILIO INNOCENTIA.

Meyer, seated on the doorstep of the house, and with, his long legs doubled up so that his knees reached his chin, no sooner perceived the approach of Cyrino, than he precipitately arose to meet him. His face was beaming with some pleasurable excitement as though he was filled with joy and triumph.

"Oh! Senhor Doctor!" he exclaimed. "Come here and see a precious thing—a discovery—a new species, such as exists nowhere else. Do you hear? Such a bicho is worth a throne, and it was I who discovered it; even Júque did not help me, for he was lying down and sleeping. Am I not right, Senhor Pereira?"

"See," murmured the Mineiro, "what a tremendous row he makes over his 'inesect.' One would think it was at least some big animal."

Meyer again exulted with pride at his success.

"It is a new species—a new one, a new one!" he exclaimed excitedly. "It is already named—I gave it a name at once—I will show it to you. Wait an instant."

Entering the room, he quickly returned with a small tin box, which he carried with the utmost reverence, and whose cover he cautiously opened, uttering, as he did so, an involuntary cry of admiration, repeated also by Cyrino, although less enthusiastically; for, pinned to a sheet of cork and with its wings half opened as though about to flutter away, there was seen the wondrous sheen of a huge and most beautiful butterfly.

The wings were of a most marvellous colour, the upper sides being of the purest and most delicate white, while the under sides were of the most brilliant metallic blue.

Meyer pointed out that the insect represented the combination of the two most beautiful lepidoptera of the woods of Rio de Janeiro—the Laertes and the Adonis, the latter showing blues equal to the purest tints of the heavens, the former being as purely white as the petals of a lily.

Without contestation, it was a most beautiful specimen, a wonderful caprice of the splendid nature of those regions. In the very exuberance of his contentment, Meyer could not keep quiet a moment.

"This butterfly," said he, as if his listeners were two professors of the science, "belongs to the family of Papilionidae, or swallow-tails, and I at once denominated it Papilio Innocentia, in honour of the daughter of Senhor Pereira, who has treated me so well. I have every respect for the great Linnaeus (Meyer raised his hand to his head in a salutation), but his classification is already a little ancient. The class is therefore Diurna, the order Lepidoptera, the genus Papilio, and the species Innocentia—my species, and which no one can rob me of. I will write from here, even to-day, to the Entomological Society of Magdeburg, and acquaint them with the fact."

Meyer delivered these sentences in an absolute tone of boastfulness, and with a slowness truly dogmatical. Afterwards, regardless of his linguistical mistakes in Portuguese—which, for the convenience of the readers, we have almost always avoided repeating—he continued with even more volubility:

"My Senhores! With the eyes of science observe this lepidoptera. It has four legs for walking; the antennae, with

CHAPTER XXI: THE PAPILIO INNOCENTIA.

long and oval terminations hollowed in the form of spoons; the eyes, larger than the head and scaly; the sucker, all white, with scarcely any lips. I lost even nothing of its fluffy for only a grain of it is worth, as much as the feather of a bird; and the comparison is perfect, for we see that each one of these scales, as in a feather, is traversed by a trachea, through which circulates the air. Oh! what a find it is!" he continued. "What a glory for me! The Entomological Society of Magdeburg ought indeed to be very proud. Without doubt, they will call a special extraordinary meeting. Mein Gott! I can hardly contain myself for joy! In two or three days more I shall be leaving this house."

"Really?" anxiously inquired Pereira.

"Yes, sir. With this discovery I am perfectly satisfied. My route will now be towards Camapuan. Afterwards I shall go to Miranda, and perhaps on to Nioac. I shall have to ascend the Rio Coxim, and thence embark for Cuyaba or go by land to Pequiry."

"And will the Senhor then return to his own country?"

"Certainly! A year and a half hence I hope to present my collections to the Entomological Society, all arranged in order."

"Man," observed Pereira, with a meaning that his guest could not possibly in the least perceive, "I long to see that day. A year and a half hence, what changes the world will show!"

"I shall have traversed," Meyer gravely replied, "eighteen signs of the zodiac."

"Very well, that is just what I want to see. That day I am impatient for, it already delays."

"When it arrives," continued the German, with some emotion and true sincerity, "I shall think with gratitude of the treatment I received in the Sertões of this Empire, and I shall have to tell—aloud, so that all can hear—that the Brazilians—are—are kind and good, for they are endued with good morals and a kindly nature."

"Just also add," interrupted Pereira, with some bitterness, "and they watch with every care over the honour of their families"

Meyer docilely obeyed, and repeated word for word:

"And they watch with every care over the honour of their families."

"Very good," grimly replied the Mineiro, "say that, and the Senhor will have said the truth."

CHAPTER XXII: MEYER DEPARTS.

In the meanwhile, the arrival of the sick and infirm, who, from many leagues around, had come to consult Cyrino, had not ceased, and so many were the cases of intermittent fever for which he had had to prescribe, that for some time past his stock of quinine had been exhausted, and he had been obliged to substitute for it the employment of certain indigenous plants of the campos and some dried herbs which he had received from some Bolivian quacks, men whom he had encountered on his travels in Minas Geraes, who had journeyed from Santa Cruz de la Sierra with the view of treating the sick people of the interior of Brazil.

Amongst the infirm, who daily arrived in quest of Cyrino, some complained of ailments which were completely unknown to him; such, for instance, as those designated the "swallow" sickness, the fallen spine, the halting sickness, the dog's cough, incurable wounds, &c. He who complained of the swallow sickness ('mal de engasgue') was the owner of a fazenda called Vão, a good two hundred miles away.

"Senhor Doctor," said the invalid, "my life is one continual struggle with suffering. On St. Johns's day, I shall have had this complaint five years. For a long time I have been unable to swallow anything without first drinking a few drops of water, and I become so wearied with everything that I am always restlessly moving from one place to another."

"Do you feel any pain?" inquired Cyrino.

"Always," replied the fazendeiro. "What troubles me most is, that though famishing with hunger, yet, in the midst of food, I cannot get any beyond my mouth. It is a fast in punishment for my sins. No sooner do I put anything, no matter how small, into my mouth, than my throat feels as if there were a big ball running up and down it."

The "medico" absolutely failed in this, as in many others, to diagnose the complaint, and prescribed some doses of the innocent "sailors' herb" (herva de marinheiro), and tendered some advice to which, the infirm one most religiously listened.

The unhappy young man thus filled up his time in the curing, or the attempting to cure, all the sick and infirm who came to him from far and near, yet he himself needed, as much as any of them, a cure for his sickness of mind.

He sorrowfully witnessed the preparations of Meyer for departure, and on the eve of leaving him, Cyrino, alone with Pereira. The latter at last had begun to see the delusion under which he had laboured; and, as the medical practice of his guest was all but exhausted, he had already suggested to Cyrino the advisability of removing himself to some other region and to continue his projected tour. All this, added to the increased fervour of his passion, served to utterly destroy the young man's peace, to emaciate his frame, and consume him as with a slow fire.

Meyer, since the finding of the magnificent butterfly, had thought only of his departure.

"Oh!" said he, "would that already I were in Magdeburg. But what a distance it is! What leagues away! Ah! Papilio Innocentia. Thou art indeed my glory! What say you, Senhor Cyrino?"

"It is true. But who knows, if the Senhor were to remain here a

CHAPTER XXII: MEYER DEPARTS.

little longer, perhaps he might find yet another new butterfly?"

"No, that is impossible. That would be too much happiness. Besides, my money will not last out."

"I can lend you some."

"Thank you very much, but to stop here any longer is altogether impossible. Do you see, I have yet to go on to Camapuan, to Miranda, to Cuyaba, and thence return, and I have only a few months in which to do it all. The Entomological Society of Magdeburg count upon seeing me in the spring of the coming year."

Once that this idea entered the mind of Meyer, he ceased not for an instant to talk of his departure, and in order to put into execution his intentions, on the afternoon of the following day he sent José Pinho to load up the mules, a proceeding which he inspected with every care.

At this moment José Pinho judged it expedient to lodge a formal protest.

"Mochu," said he, "is about to recommence his mode of travelling these roads at night. I know it will only end in our tumbling down some precipice, I, the Senhor, the mules, the loads, and the bichos, and neither shall I arrive in Rio de Janeiro nor he in his country. Well, I am already tired of warning him. I have said my say, and. there's an end of it."

On the occasion of the departure, the naturalist presented that same aspect which he showed on the day of his arrival. There was the same array of flasks and other appendages attached to his cross-belt, the same queer costume, that same tranquil air and good-natured expression as when, at midnight, he sought the hospitality of Pereira.

This latter individual, on seeing his guest mounted and ready to leave the homestead for ever, was filled with joy; at the same time, with the admiration he felt for the German, he could not conquer a certain internal disturbance of feeling. In the depths of his conscience, he commenced to doubt if his apprehensions had not been ill-founded, and for the moment he allowed himself to be carried away by the sympathy which the mild and naturally inoffensive character of the Saxon produced upon all who knew him.

"The hour has arrived," declared Meyer, and clasping with a firm and honest grasp the hand of Pereira, "Senhor Pereira," said he, "adieu! Never more shall we meet again, yet I shall think of you all my life. When I am in my country, thousands and thousands of leagues away—my memory will recall the happy days I passed here."

"Oh! Senhor Meyer," stammered Pereira.

"Yes, indeed happy days," continued Meyer very slowly. "Happy, for they passed away without my perceiving the lapse of time. This house, your home, will, above all others in Brazil, be ever the most vivid and brightest spot in my

CHAPTER XXII: MEYER DEPARTS.

recollections."

In order to emphasise the force of his convictions, the German struck his clenched fist in the open palm of the other hand, and then, turning to Cyrino, he added:

"Senhor Doctor, your prescriptions are all entered in my note-book. Sometimes you make mistakes, it is true, but as your intentions are always for the best, that will excuse them. I — —"

Interrupting what he was about to say, he paused a few seconds to wistfully gaze at Pereira and Cyrino, who were equally silent; a long tear trickled down his face, but without in the least disturbing his otherwise placid physiognomy.

"Adieu my friends!" he suddenly uttered.

"A good journey to you, Senhor Meyer! a good journey to you," joyfully replied Pereira.

"Adieu! Adieu!" repeated Meyer, and then addressing his man, "Júque," said he; "Go on in front. Be gentle with the little mule. We shall rest about half a league hence."

Meyer then seized the reins and proceeded at a walking pace behind José Pinho, who was armed with a stout staff evidently intended to be used on the quarters of the mule committed to his care.

"There goes the bicho!" exclaimed Pereira, on seeing the tails of the little troop. "Ah! What a relief it is to be sure! Yet after all, poor fellow, he was not a bad sort; but he had no manners, you know. Phew! All my life long I shall never forget that Meyer! It *was* a campaign. Wah! Look, Senhor Cyrino! Is he not returning? Has he forgotten anything?"

The German was indeed returning, and he seemed to be in

search of, or about to say, something of importance.

"Well, what is it?" inquired Pereira, raising his voice. "Have you left something behind? You must look sharp, for it will be dark soon."

As Meyer approached, he replied, "I have left nothing, Senhor Pereira, but I omitted to perform a duty."

"What is that?" inquired the Mineiro.

"I did not say good-bye to your daughter."

"Oh! don't trouble yourself about that," Pereira hastily replied. "It is not at all necessary; besides, she is now sleeping, and is not very well. She complained of a headache a short time ago. I will tell her what you say."

"Well then," observed Meyer very gravely, "tell her, that wherever I may be, she will always find in me a willing servant and a sincere friend. For ever her name will be known to science, and by me will be remembered as long as I live, for the esteem I have for her is very great. She is really a most beautiful girl, and should rather be an ornament to European society than one of the neglected wild flowers of the campos."

"Certainly, certainly," interrupted Pereira. "Go, go without fear."

"Yes, I will go. Adieu, my friends."

"Go then at once, for look you, the sun is sinking behind yonder wood, and night soon will fall."

"Yes, yes. Adieu! Adieu!" the German repeated, and finally went on his way.

Along the far-extending sandy road the shadow of the good Meyer, as he marched onwards behind his man, his pack-

CHAPTER XXII: MEYER DEPARTS.

mule, and collections, became longer and longer in the rays of the setting sun.

CHAPTER XXIII: THE LAST INTERVIEW.

After the departure of Meyer, Pereira returned to sleep at night in the rear, or that part of the house reserved as the sanctuary of the family, and as he also passed the greater part of his time there, any further meetings of the two lovers seemed absolutely impossible; besides this, his attention, no longer having the object to which it had been constantly directed during the stay of the German, commenced to return to Cyrino, to whom he confessed he had treated Meyer with unmerited opprobrium.

"Now," said the Minciro, "my conscience really pains me for the way I treated that man. Who knows if all I thought was only an illusion of my mind? Ah, Senhor Cyrino, when people begin to get suspicious they are on the way to get fooled. Yes, sir, I am now convinced that the German was a good and sincere man. He saw the girl and found her pretty, and then uttered all that bundle of nonsense, without meaning any harm by it. He who says what he thinks is he who can be trusted. Sometimes the danger comes from whence we least expect. Well, after all, I do not repent very much for doing what I have done. I had reason to fear, and accordingly I took precautions."

These and similar remarks furnished ample occasion for reflection on the part of Cyrino. From any one hour to another he well knew that the inquisitorial views of his host might be directed to himself and render his position untenable.

Meanwhile he sought to procure another interview with Innocencia. Great were the difficulties that lay in the way, and

CHAPTER XXIII: THE LAST INTERVIEW.

the only means that offered was to seek a renewal of the nocturnal meetings, and thus, during many successive nights, he passed his vigils in the orange-grove, watching with steadfast eyes the window of Innocencia's room. Finally, one night, just before dawn, his patience was rewarded, for then at last he perceived at the window the figure of his well-beloved.

In an instant he was with. Her, and, eagerly grasping- her hands, he exclaimed, "At last! At last! I am with, you!"

"My father may awaken," whispered the girl, so softly that her words were hardly more audible thian the murmur of the night breeze.

"I care not," Cyrino hoarsely replied; "let him discover all; I can exist like this no longer."

"Hush-sh!" she observed; "take care; if he finds us here he will kill us both. Listen; go and wait for me close to the stream by the orange-grove; in a little while I will be with Mecê. The door is not fastened."

The young man made signs that he would obey, and incontinently disappeared amidst the shadows of the orange-trees.

At that hour the gleams of a waning moon spread a feeble light upon the land, seeming as the forerunner of another and stronger light, about to irradiate with all its splendour the yet sleeping nature, and inspire it with coming animation and joy. Amidst the branches of the orange-trees were heard the rustle of birds about to awake; here and there a suppressed warble or chirrup, or the flutter of a wing, while afar off an early-rising thrush trilled his notes—a clear and harmonious sound amidst the silence of the hour. In the east a faint crimson flush announced the first glimmer of dawn amidst the fading lights of the starry heavens. In the west, encircled by a broad and yellowish aureola, yet lingered the pale moon.

Cyrino was so agitated that he was obliged to seat himself whilst awaiting the approach of Innocencia.

She delayed not long. She came clad in a short-skirted dress of coarse cotton cloth, her head enveloped in a mantle of the same material, the folds of which her hands clasped to her neck. Her feet were bare, and the firm manner in which she trod the thorn and pine-strewn ground showed that they were well habituated to such rough treatment, yet withal, in nowise had they lost any of their primitive elegance and delicacy of form.

She seemed terribly frightened, and her eyes filled with tears.

The youth, immediately he saw her, rushed forward to meet her.

"Innocencia," he exclaimed, on noting a trembling gesture of fear, "fear nothing from me. I shall respect you as if you were a saint. Do you not then confide in me?"

"Yes!" she hastily replied. "Otherwise I would not have come, but, nevertheless, my face is burning with shame— —" And carrying one of the hands of Cyrino to her cheeks she continued, "Feel, Cyrino, how my face is a very fire. Oh! why is it that Mecê comes to disturb me so? Before this I was a happy contented girl, but now—ah! if Mecê cares for me no more—ah, me! I fear I shall die!"

"No! no!" the young man earnestly exclaimed. "If on that depends your life, then, indeed, you will live to eternity.'"

"Really?"

"I swear to you, it is easier to suddenly extinguish the light of

CHAPTER XXIII: THE LAST INTERVIEW.

all yonder stars than that I could cease to love thee——"

"But Manecão?" she suggested in a voice of terror.

"Ah! That man. Ever that cursed name!"

"But he will be my husband——"

"That,;never, Innocencia! It is impossible! Everything may happen except that. And if we fly? Listen! To-morrow at this hour, or even earlier, I will bring here two good animals; you shall mount one, I the other; then we will speed onwards towards S. Anna, and by constantly galloping we will soon reach Uberaba, where we will find a padre to marry us. Let us go. Do you hear?"

"And will Mecê esteem me all his life?"

"Ay, that would I, if it lasted for ever. Say yes, for the 'Amor de Deus.' Speak, and we are saved!"

"And my father, Cyrino? Oh! what is to be done? He would curse me. I should be a lost woman—an abandoned woman—without the blessing of a father. No! Mecê is tempting me—No! I will not fly—rather would I suffer misery all my life, but then I shall always be what my name says I am, although so sinful in doing what I do. Mecê is a young man from the cities, and thinks nothing of deceiving such a poor girl as I. Even ——"

"Very well," interrupted Cyrino. "It is then decided. You will not go with me. Let us say no more about it. I want to do nothing except such as you consider good, and if finally I decide to speak to your father——"

"Heaven protect us!" she ejaculated. "I thought at first that it might be, but afterwards I saw that it would only make things worse. Mecê knows not what means the word of a Mineiro;

iron breaks, but that never—Manecão will have to be his son-in-law."

"Who knows, Innocencia? I will beg, pray, and entreat, with such humility— —"

"Pshaw! What vain hopes! They will serve you nothing."

"Then what can be done?" cried the young man in despair. "To what saint can we appeal? Why is it that Heaven sends us such misery?" And burying his face in his hands, the youth wept bitterly.

Innocencia on her part laid her head on the shoulders of her lover, and both cried like the children they really were. She was the first to break the silence.

"Ah! meu Deus! if my godfather wished— —"

"Your godfather?" inquired Cyrino. "Who is he?"

"He is a man who lives away there by Paranahybas, in the region of the Geraes."

"Where? Is it far?"

"It is some distance, not very near. Does Mecê know the Senhor Padua?"

"I know him. He lives about sixty-four miles from the Rio Paranahyba."

"Well, that is where my godfather lives, to the left of the fazenda of Padua, on some lands received from the government."

"And how is he called?"

"Antonio Cesario. My father is indebted to him for money and does anything he orders. If he says but the word Manecão will

CHAPTER XXIII: THE LAST INTERVIEW.

find himself baffled."

"Oh!" exclaimed Cyrino excitedly. "Then we are saved! To-morrow I will mount and ride there. From here to the town is only twenty-eight miles, and to there about sixty-eight. It is merely an excursion—I arrive—I tell him all—and then follow my trail to your feet, and——"

"But," interrupted Innocencia, "do not mention me, do you hear? Say nothing about having arranged anything with me. I have nothing to do with it, do you understand? or else everything will be lost. Invent some story—make out that you are rich—do not let him imagine that it was I who bid you knock at his door. Ah me! with suspicious people one has to know how to negotiate."

"Ah! meu Deus!" exclaimed Cyrino, in an ecstasy of joy, "we are saved! There is no doubt of it. I see now how everything must happen. After a day or two's stay with him I will disclose everything, then the old man writes a letter to your father, and, if it does not remove Manecão at once, it will at least gain time. I am already anxious to be mounted on my old mule and on the road. Two days to go, two to return, and two or three to stop there, in more or less than a week I shall be back again, bringing with me my happiness or my misery. No! I have faith in Nossa Senhora de Abbadia. She will help us, and together we shall yet fulfil the promises we have made her."

"What promises?" inquired Innocencia, with curiosity.

"That we shall go on foot from here to the town and place two blessed candles on the altar of Nossa Senhora."

"Yes!" earnestly replied the girl, "I swear I will—even if it were to go to the end of the world."

"Oh! my saint of Paradise!" exclaimed Cyrino, as he clasped the girl to his breast. "Ah! how I love thee!"

Thus they remained embraced in each other's arms while day slowly dawned in the firmament, and rays of undecided light fell upon the earth as if seeking to sound the depths of darkness. The birds softly twittered and chirruped, preparing their little throats for the matutinal concert, and the dew of night, ascending in filmy clouds to the heavens, moistened the foliage of the trees and jewelled the points of the grasses and dwarf vegetation with jems that glistened like diamonds.

Far away, by the borders of some stream, the macaws screeched with harsh but sonorous cries, and the macuan sent over the solitudes the prolonged notes of his brazen throat.

"It is day," observed Innocencia, withdrawing herself from the arms of Cyrino.

"Already!" he regretfully exclaimed.

"MeuDeus, and I have yet to return to the house—I must go now."

"Then I will depart even to-day," said the young man.

"Yes, do."

"And in the coming week I will be back again."

"Very well. Take with you this certainty, that my life or my death depends on my godfather."

"And mine also," replied the youth, fervently kissing her hands.

"Leave me—leave me," she implored. "Adieu! Ah! I am so fearful! Happily no one has seen me. Ah! Listen——"

At this moment, and as if in response to the assertion, there

CHAPTER XXIII: THE LAST INTERVIEW.

sounded from the orange-grove that same sharp whistle which had so startled the two lovers on the first of their meetings.

Innocencia trembled so violently that she nearly fell to the ground. "Meu Deus!" she stammered. "It is an omen of warning. But who knows if it is not some human being?"

The whistle was followed by a kind of mocking laughter which froze the blood in the veins of the lovers. The girl, in a tremor of fright, clutched Cyrino by his arms.

"It is a soul from the other world," she murmured, as she crossed herself.

The youth, however, maintained his presence of mind, and, invoking the aid of S. Miguel, he made the sign of the Cross in the direction of the four cardinal points, then, supporting the girl in his arms, he hastily crossed the orchard and left her close to the half-opened back door of the house, which he thought had been blown open by the wind.

Innocencia nearly fainted, but, gathering her strength, she was enabled to enter the house, and, with a cautious but trembling hand, drew the bolt inside.

As soon as he was thus assured of her safety, Cyrino hurried back to the orchard, and, as before, he again commenced to traverse it in every direction, seeking to discover, in the dawning light of day, whether it was some human being or else some ghostly phantom who thus was sporting with him.

Just as he was about to pass by a densely-foliaged orange-tree, he suddenly perceived amidst the boughs above him a dark, ill-defined form which immediately descended and almost fell upon him, amidst a shower of broken twigs and branches, and as it struck the ground, it uttered a strange unearthly cry.

"Holy Cross! Avaunt thee, fiend!" cried the young man, and, phantom-like, a small creature passed between his legs and disappeared amid the yet dark shadows of the trees.

Cyrino remained still with hair on end, eyes fixed, and limbs paralysed with fright, his dry lips stuttering an exorcism, and his legs trembling as if they were green saplings quivering in the wind. A voice some distance away recalled him to his senses. It was that of Pereira, who, with his hands forming a trumpet to his mouth, was shouting to one of his slaves.

"Fire, José!" he exclaimed. "If it is some soul of the other world or a wolf- man[40] the ball will not harm him, but if it is anything human, so much the better. Fire!"

The report of a gun followed, and a ball, whistling by the ears of Cyrino, buried itself in the trunk of a tree close by.

The young man waited not for another, and, favoured by the yet prevalent obscurity, he hurried away in the direction of the front of the house, and had barely entered the guests' room when Pereira appeared at the door.

"What was that?" Cyrino inquired, as with a strong effort he composed his countenance.

"I don't know," responded the Mineiro. "There was a hurly-burly of squeals and squawls at daybreak that sounded like a lot of hobgoblins fresh from inferno. The little one was in such a state of terror that I thought she would die of fright. I believe it was the soul of 'the collector'[41] peowling round the house.

---

[40]A wolf-man (Lobishomen) is a creation of Brazilian superstition.—[Transl.]

[41]This collector of whom Pereira spoke, and whose soul is said by the Sertanejos to wander about the region of Sant'Anna de Paranahyba, was a public *employé*, who was prosecuted and imprisoned, after being convicted of felony in the discharge of his duties. He died in prison, and, as the State sequestrated all his belongings, his excellent homestead fell into abandonment and ruin.

CHAPTER XXIII: THE LAST INTERVIEW.

May it not be an omen of evil? The Senhora Sant'Anna protect us."

"Well, I slept like a lump of lead," said Cyrino unblushingly. "The report of your shot awoke me."

"Well, you can't drop off again now, because in an instant or two the sun will be up and give us broad daylight."

CHAPTER XXIV: THE TOWN OF SANT'ANNA.

The same day Cyrino mounted his mule, and, on taking leave of Pereira, informed him that he would be absent for a week more or less, giving as a reason for so unexpected a journey, not only the necessity of visiting some distant patients but also of procuring some remedies which be required.

From the house of Pereira to that of Albino Lata the road is so shady and pleasant that these twelve miles were easily covered. From here, however, commence the open and rolling grass lands of the campos, extending over a distance of sixteen miles, close to the town of Sant'Anna; and, under the ardent rays of the mid-day sun, they are a somewhat weary stretch for the traveller, especially one with a troubled mind, for physical inconvenience only augments mental irritation.

As Cyrino passed over those sandy plains, weltering in the scorching heat of the sun, all the hopefulness which had buoyed him up as he wended his way through the soft shades of the first part of the road now seemed to disappear, and give place to a disconsolate and forlorn sense of despair of a happy exit out of the doubts surrounding the motive of his journey. Dejected and pale with anxiety, he allowed the reins of his animal to fall upon its neck, and it to proceed at a slow pace—in sympathy, as it were, with the dolorous forebodings of its rider.

"What shall I do?" he thought to himself. "How shall I broach the subject?"

So great was his despondency that he almost arrived at the pitch of cursing the beloved one of his heart.

CHAPTER XXIV: THE TOWN OF SANT'ANNA.

"Unhappy was the hour when first I saw that woman! Otherwise I could have gone on my way in peace. But now—ah! her eyes haunt me and lead me on to destruction—a beckoning: finger, that, whether I will or not, I must follow even if it leads me to—Yet, ah! Innocencia," he exclaimed, in a contrite voice, "pardon me, Innocencia, my angel. I am even cursing the hour of the birth of my happiness—I, who can fly if I would; but you, a prisoner in your home! No! Unhappy me, I alone am to blame."

Thus steeped in melancholy thought he arrived at the town of Sant'Anna de Paranahyba.

From a distance, the aspect of the town is picturesque in the extreme. On the edge of the wild moorlands of the Sertão of Mato Grosso, and situated on the spur of a low range of hills, it rises up above, and overlooks, the surrounding plains. That, however, which gives it such an especial charm to any one seeing it from afar, is the appearance of the vast orange-groves surrounding the town, and yearly crowned with thousands of golden fruit, and amidst which are dotted the white-walled and red-tiled houses of the town, while, high above the dark green foliage of the trees, rises the cross of the modest church.

Crossing a brook of gurgling limpid waters, and ascending a stony ascent, lined right and left by little adobe-walled houses and palm-leaf or straw-thatched huts, one reaches the principal street, whose most prominent feature is a spacious old-fashioned house of two stories. An iron verandah extends the whole length of the front, over which the roof projects in a motherly sort of way as if it would shelter the whole house from the torrid rays of the sun.

It was here that resided the Major Martinho de Mello Taques, and in his dry goods store on the ground floor were accustomed to congregate all the gossips of the place to discuss politics and local scandals.

In that silent street, which impresses one so forcibly as the melancholy type of a decadent centre of a decadent population, the prevailing monotony would be now and then disturbed by the clouds of dust raised by the arrival of a mule-troop, an incident which would attract to every window the lean, sallow faces of women, or to the doors the pallid forms of children, pot-bellied from the habit of earth-eating or the fevers of the Rio Paranahyba. Also on Sundays, at the hour of mass, would congregate many old women, enveloped in mantilhas, and accompanied by other younger females, clad in long black cloaks reaching to their heels, and wearing the high combs so fashionable in years gone by.

Cyrino rode through the town, and, as he passed the residence of the major he waved a salutation to that individual, as he did not intend to stop to speak to him.

The major, as usual, was seated on his counter, and, surrounded by the *élite* of the society of the place, he was recounting to them many an oft-told tale—not only his own exploits, but also those of the old pioneers of the Sertão, anecdotes which were ever ready at the tip of his tongue.

"There goes the doctor," said one of those present.

"Halloa, Senhor Cyrino!" shouted the major, running to the doorway; "what is it that brings you here? What is your hurry? Stop a moment, won't you?"

Cyrino pulled up his animal at these words.

"The truth is," said he, "I am on a journey, but not a very long one. I shall probably be back again in eight or ten days."

CHAPTER XXIV: THE TOWN OF SANT'ANNA.

The whole human contents of the store had by this time sallied out to the street, where the youth was at once surrounded by the little crowd of idle gossips, some almost treading on the hoofs of the mule, others stroking its neck or playing with the reins, as their idle fancy induced them, while each one pressed forward with curiosity depicted on his or her face.

The major comprehended the situation at a glance.

"Every one has his own private affairs to attend to," he observed, by way of commencement of an inquisition, "but, if it is no secret, what the diabo signifies this return here?"

"He ought to be far away from here now," observed one man. "It is nearly two months since be left— —"

"Wait," interrupted the padre of the town; "it is not so, it is not yet two months. The doctor passed along this very street just one month and twenty-two days ago at eight o'clock in the morning.

"Very well, then," continued the major, "he has already had more than enough time to be out there by Miranda."

"That is if I was travelling light," replied Cyrino; "but you see I have baggage mules, and besides, I stop here and there to treat the sick."

"Ah! truly!" confirmed the collector (a long lanky man wearing an old-fashioned tall 'chimney-pot' silk hat). "They do not think of that. All they think about is talk—talk— —"

"I hope you do not refer to me," interrupted the padre in an irascible tone.

"Whoever thought of doing so, Senhor Padre?" hastily protested the other. "I speak in general, in general, you know,

I do not— —"

"But, doctor," the major cut in, "where have you been staying all this time? In some fazenda, eh?"

As the cross-examination promised to last some time, it was absolutely necessary to devise some means to stop it.

"I have already been close to Sucuriu," said Cyrino, somewhat perturbed, "in the— —"

"It is not so very near as that," observed the padre. "Once I
— —"

"Now listen, Senhor Padre," ejaculated the collector, who showed signs of some long-standing antagonism to the priest. "The young man never said it might be close to *here*."

The major repeated the words of Cyrino, somewhat accentuating them. "Then the Senhor Doctor has been nearly close to Sucuriu? Is it not so?"

"It is a fact. There I met a person who, for some time, has owed me some money."

"Some money?" inquired the padre. "A person? What person? Who might it be now, eh?"

"Now whoever can it be?" chorused a few voices.

The major implacably proceeded: "Let the doctor explain. You people make quite an 'algazarra'" (a shout, a noise).[42]

Almost stammering, Cyrino sought to continue:

"Yes—it was a muleteer—he sent to me an order to receive payment—from—from a relative; I also had to pay the—the

---

[42]This word has been left in because it is interesting to see how such a distinctly Moorish word is yet used by country Brazilians in the backwoods of the Empire, for "algazarra" was the war-cry of the Moors.—[Transl.]

CHAPTER XXIV: THE TOWN OF SANT'ANNA.

other person—that—that— —"

"Wait a moment," interrupted the major; "then you had to receive money and pay it back, eh? Is it not all the same thing?"

"Why of course it is," added several of the bystanders.

Cyrino abruptly ceased his explanations.

"Well," said he, "I shall be very soon returning here. I have to go a little beyond the river there."

"Do you go to Melancia?" inquired the collector, haphazardly using the name of a well-known halting place for travellers.

"Further on," responded the young man, who, seeing the utter impossibility of honourably evading the examination, altered his tactics, and addressing the major, said, "On my return I shall have to purchase some sheeting and calicoes of you."

"Ha! ha! I knew it," boisterously ejaculated the padre. "The doctor is going to get married."

"Ho! ho!" observed some one. "Why so much secrecy? No one wants to rob him of his bride."

"Above all," pondered the padre, "when the business has to go through my hands."

The sudden reserve and the silence of Cyrino which followed these remarks gave occasion, for the moment, to many observations.

"I congratulate you," said one man.

"But who is the fortunate one of the Sertão?" inquired others.

"Meus Senhors," cried the youth, seeking to rebuke the assumption. "It is nothing at all."

The padre, however, proceeded: "If you want a bit of advice, just hurry, for then I shall be able to knock over two rabbits with one blow of a stick, that is, if I marry the Senhor and the Manecão at the same time."

"Ah! so you can," cried several of the men.

"But where has he got to?" asked another.

"A short while ago be was here."

"Who? Manecão?"

"Yes."

"Halloa! Here be comes," announced a third. And really, at the end of the road, a man was seen approaching, mounted on a fiery horse, whose violent movements be calmly controlled with a firm and steady band.

The new-comer was quite the type of a captain of muleteers. The long, flowing black hair, the wild yet gloomy expression, the sunburnt visage, and the vigorous, lithe muscular form, formed a whole that at once would attract attention. Hat, jacket; and leggings were of tanned deerskin; a red handkerchief hung loosely round his neck; his bare feet, carrying huge spurs, rested in coal-scuttle-shaped brass stirrups; the holsters of his saddle showed the buts of long horse-pistols; and a bone-handle whip in his hand completed the *tout-ensemble* of a muleteer in the exercise of his functions.

"Nosso Senhor be with you," he curtly observed, as he reined in his steed in front of the group and lightly touched the brim of his hat with the point of a forefinger.

"Good-day to you, Senhor Manecão," replied the major on behalf of his companions, "or rather good afternoon. I know already that you are on the way to be done for."

CHAPTER XXIV: THE TOWN OF SANT'ANNA.

"Without doubt," croaked the padre, "he is going to see the little torment."

The muleteer grimly smiled as he replied:

"No fear, Senhor Vicar, I am not going to be demoralised by any woman; but a man is not a mule; some day he must have a child of his own. Life is but a journey"

Cyrino and Manecão, the two prominent figures amidst the group of idle gossips, presented extreme contrasts. One, so lusty in his rude health, so proud and indifferent in his bearing, as he calmly gazed around him; the other quite pallid, and trembling with nervousness.

"Is this owl the surgeon?" inquired Manecão, in a low voice; glancing at Cyrino, as he leaned forward to address the collector. "Clotildes of the Venda, up town, told me he had arrived. To me, he seems to have the face of a humbug."

"Eh, man," retorted the other, "but he has got a head on his shoulders. He has made a heap of cures about here."

Cyrino, noting that he was the subject of observation, with an amiable smile saluted his rival:

"Good even' to you, my countryman."

"Oh! Life to you," the muleteer drily and sharply replied, and glancing towards the sun, added: "See here now, what it is to be like a woman clacking her tongue. The sun is sinking, and I have yet to cover a lot of ground. Friends, adieu! Senhor Major until I see you again—Senhor Vicar, I shall shortly be here." Spurring his animal, the circle of gossips quickly scattered, and Manecão proceeded on his way at a fast pace.

Cyrino in his turn, utilising the rupture of the ring that had heretofore encircled him, pressed the hand of the major and went away in the direction of the Rio Paranahyba, on whose margins he expected to pass the night. Hardly had he disappeared when a perfect rain of comments on him was poured out by the gossips.

"Did you notice," said the vicar to the major, "how the doctor is altered? So pale and old he looks! eh?

"Now I don't think he does," contradicted the collector, "I really do not."

The Senhor Taques, major and justice of the peace, assumed an air of profound meditation, and with an extended finger slowly pointing upwards he gravely apostrophized:

"Mark my words, Senhores, hereabouts you will see by-and-by the 'tooth of a rabbit![43]'"

During that night and many subsequent days the town repeated those celebrated words.

"It was the major who said so," every one asseverated in a tone of conviction, "we shall see the tooth of a rabbit."

---

[43] A provincialism expressive of mischief or trouble [Transl.]

CHAPTER XXV: THE JOURNEY.

In little more than an hour Cyrino traversed the distance between the town and the river, for, in the five miles that it measures, the only bad bit of road is that which passes through the wooded margins of the majestic stream. In this forest, the vestiges of great floods are seen on the trunks of the trees, and the soft and swampy soil is a hotbed of vegetable putrefaction, whence, on the occasion of the intense heat that follows retreat of the waters, proceeds deadly miasma.

Here, by the gloomy margins of pestiferous pools of stagnant and slime-covered water, the dwarf and heavily-foliaged aucury palms are found in abundance. The aspect is in no way agreeable, and the thought that here is the haunt and home of the terrible marsh fevers serves to cause any passing traveller to hasten away from these lugubrious regions.

The murmur of the flow of water is heard at a short distance from the shores of the river. The stream is wide, its waters clear, and the current flows rapidly.

On the glistening surface of the river are reflected the two green borders of its elevated banks, where many a tottering tree, with its foundations undermined by floods, and balancing continually to and fro, causes a constant gentle ripple.

The contemplation of such an imposing mass of water—rolling, ever rolling onwards, as if by some hidden power—causes an involuntary feeling of depression.

As when the ocean, with its incessant monotonous movement, agitates the soul, so also does that perennial flow. The impressive silence of an immense river induces us insensibly to meditation. And when a man meditates, he saddens.

Joy is naturally the frank and spontaneous accompaniment of all expanding nature. Sadness is a vague metaphysical aspiration, an innately restless, painful craving for action; its home, the silent depths of the forest or the desert solitude. No one prepares to become merry, while, on the other hand, melancholy comes not suddenly, and the result of the psychological phenomenon is that each is linked to the other.

How did that enormous mass of water spring into existence? From whence comes it? Whither is it bound? What mysteries are not buried in its bosom?

Cyrino remained for a long time gazing at the river, while dark thoughts surged through his mind. Twilight was creeping on, and, as the last rays of the sun tinged with rosy hues the tops of the loftiest trees, numerous flocks of noisy quero-queros saluted the departing light of day, and awoke the echoes with their discordant cries. Occasionally a wild duck would pass by with heavy laboured flight, white herons skimmed the surface of the waters with outstretched snowy wings, and hundreds of wood pigeons crossed from bank to bank, homeward bound to their well-known haunts.

As the waning light gradually disappeared and darkness quickly followed, the river assumed an uniform tint, like unto a sheet of burnished silver.

"Ah! well, now know I thee, Manecão!" thought Cyrino, heaving a sigh. "And for such as he is reserved my gentle Innocencia! Humph. Truly a pretty man—for me, for her, a horrid monster. Yet how strong he is!"

Without casting any disparagement upon the courage of our hero, it was certainly evident that the physical strength of his

CHAPTER XXV: THE JOURNEY.

rival was a source of irritation to Cyrino. "Ah!" he muttered, "if I could—crush him! How dark and foreboding he looked! Meu Deus! Give me courage—give me hopes. Nossa Senhora de Abbadia! Nossa Senhora da Canna Verde!—aid me!"

Amidst all the wild surroundings of those immense scenes of nature, and oppressed with the passion that raged within his breast, the youth fell upon his knees, praying with fervour, or rather automatically stringing together the simple prayers which his mother had taught him when a child.

The river flowed onwards serenely, while far away a jaguar roared, and some night-bird suddenly startled the silence of the night with a strange, piercing cry.

* * * * *

Crossing the river on the following morning, Cyrino trod the territory of Minas Geraes, and, after traversing some six miles of forest, he entered upon a far-extending rolling campos-land, a region somewhat burnt with the sun and extremely monotonous in aspect, but abounding with quail and partridges.

So immersed in thought was the young man, that he never once attempted to imitate the prolonged wailing notes of the birds which resounded from all sides, an impulse which always prompts those who travel in those regions.

With ever-rising impatience he thought of the sixty-four miles which yet separated him from the fazenda of Padua. His heart was heavy with sadness, and his eyes filled with tears every time he contemplated a burity palm, for then his thoughts flew to the home of Innocencia, where, close to the margin of the stream, where he had had his last interview, arose one of these stately palms, the queen of the Sertão. Of what is the dear one now thinking? What will happen to her? And Manecão, is he already there? At such a thought Cyrino became overwhelmed with agitation, and, briskly spurring his animal to a gallop, he rode furiously onwards.

The impassive majesty of nature oppressed him. To him, the road was transformed into a path of torments through which he craved to fly with furious velocity, yet slowly, withal, seemed to him to pass the varied landmarks of his journey.

When man suffers, in the agony of his wild arrogance, he craves to witness the savage destruction of the fury of the storm, in harmony with his tempestuous thoughts.

"Meu Deus!" murmured Cyrino, "all around joy seems to reign! The birds fly so lightly; the flowers are so beautiful; the streams so clear and peaceful that all seems to invite repose. I only suffer. Ah! surely death is better than this torment. Who can tear from my heart this weight, this certainty of misery? What after all is this love? Perhaps, years hence, I shall not even remember Innocencia. Maybe I am only uselessly torturing myself. Yet no, that woman is my life, my very blood. Who takes her from me, kills me. Well, let death come, she at least will remain to weep for me—remain to tell of a man who knew how to love." He suddenly raised his voice and shouted aloud, "Innocencia! Innocencia!" And the echoes —sweet as any sounds—repeated that dear name, as they repeat the roar of the puma, the plaintive warble of the thrush, or the strident hammering of the anvil bird.

As all things, however, have an end, on the fourth day Cyrino reached the house of Antonio Cesario, who welcomed him with all amiability and frankness, and under whose roof we will meanwhile leave him, in order see what, in Pereira's home, happened to the gentle Innocencia and those who

CHAPTER XXV: THE JOURNEY.

destined her to the sacrifice of enforced matrimony.

CHAPTER XXVI: A CORDIAL RECEPTION.

Manecão soon arrived at the house of his future father-in-law. The distance from Sant'Anna was not great, and it was quickly covered by the spirited animal which carried the muleteer, who, moreover; applied both whip and spur.

The soul of Manecão was filled with impatience, for the memory of the rarely beautiful bride awaiting him created an unaccustomed feeling of elation, and at times the habitual gloom would fly from his face and a faint smile played upon the lips and moved, as though unwillingly, the dense moustache.

Pereira received him with an explosion of absolute joy.

"Viva! viva!" he boisterously exclaimed, as he extended his arms. "Welcome, a merry welcome to this ranch! We want only music and rejoicings to celebrate your arrival! What a time you have been coming! I thought that you could not find the road to the house;. 'Nocencia will jump for very joy."

Whilst Pereira poured out these words almost in shouts, the Sertanejo dismounted, and, hat in hand, advanced to ask a blessing of his future father-in-law.

"Deus give thee His blessing," said Pereira, fervently embracing him. "Did you not want to come— —?"

"How goes the little one?" interrupted Manecão.

"She is very well now. She has had the ague, but now she is all right again."

"Has she thought of me?"

CHAPTER XXVI: A CORDIAL RECEPTION.

"Now what a question that is, when you so bewitch everybody. Why, even I, myself, have thought of nothing but you. 'When will Manecão arrive?' I was always saying to myself, and many a time I looked down the road, with longing eyes, for any signs of you. How much more then with a woman, a never-ending longing. But," he continued, "we are clattering our tongues and I have not yet made you come in. 'Nocencia has just this instant gone to the stream. Unharness your animal and leave the things here."

Manecão did as Pereira told him. He removed the saddle, not hurriedly, but carefully and slowly, and, in order that the heated animal should not take cold, he left the saddle-cloth on its back, and with a head of maize bereft of its grains he rubbed down the neck and hocks of the horse.

After completing this operation he entered the house, making it resound with the clank of the huge rowels of his spurs, which, by reason of their immense size, obliged him to walk so that his heels did not touch the ground.

The Mineiro could not contain himself in his satisfaction. "Then—then is all now arranged?" he inquired, gleefully rubbing his hands.

"Everything. All the papers are ready. I had to go to Ubereba for them, and that is what delayed me so long. When Mecê wills, we will start off for Sant'Anna. I purchased some horses, and they will be here to-morrow. I have already spoken to Lata; the vicar has received notice; the day only requires to be named."

"In that case, the sooner the better. Don't you think so?"

"Certainly it is."

"Well then, let us say on the second Sunday from now."

"As you like. As for me, you well know that, in this business of marriage, what costs most is to make theo resolution to enter it; afterwards one gets accustomed to the new life. Is the girl ready?"

"I don't know—she ought to be, for I see her always sewing something or other. However, I must fix the day, as I have sent to invite Roberto's people. Finally, it is necessary to kill the fatted pig and send to fetch aquadente. When one marries a daughter, and an only one, one has to keep his pockets pretty wide open. Everything has been arranged, the signal only is required, when all will be ready. Here in front of the house there will be a big ranch, and in the yard on the right will be another one for the dinner. In Sant'Anna I ordered the music, and Mestre Tabuco promised some pieces that will bring the tears to your eyes. Then blunderbuss and bomb shall thunder——"

"I," interrupted Manecão, "with your permission, have ordered in the store of the major two dozen bottles of wine."

"Man! You *have* gone in for expenses! Two dozen bottles of wine! Wah!"

"Sim, Senhor!"

"Well, my dear fellow, they must be looked after, that's all. We shall want them for the vicar, the major, the collector, and the schoolmaster, people of some consideration, and whom I count upon, without all the small fry, who will be without end. Ten days before the festival I want Ricardo's women to come and prepare the nicknacks, the sweets, cakes, and all that, and we must have 'chicolate'[44] ready every morning. You see how they will talk about this feast. The songs and dances we will have, eh? Ho! ho! What a festival it will be. Eh?"

---

[44] Coffee with milk, sugar, and beaten eggs.

CHAPTER XXVI: A CORDIAL RECEPTION.

"But what of your daughter?" inquired Manecão.

Pereira laughed. "Ah! You rogue, you think of nothing else, eh? Well I used to be the same—every one in his time—that is the law of Nosso Senhor Jesus Christo."

Going out into the yard, and placing his hands as a trumpet to his mouth, he shouted:

"'Nocencia! 'Nocencia!"

No reply came.

"Poor little thing," said he, "when she comes back from the stream she will be like a frightened deer." And then added, "As she does not arrive, let us go within. You are now one of us, come here and go to my own room, there you will find no want of hammocks and soft skins."

On saying- these words, Pereira amiably patted the broad shoulders of Manecão and made him enter the sacred rear precincts of the house.

CHAPTER XXVII: HUNTING THE DOE.

To describe the shock that Innocencia received on finding herself face to face with Manecão would be impossible. Alarm and terror were so strongly depicted on her countenance, that it was observed, not only by the bridegroom, but also by the father.

"What is the matter with you?" inquired Pereira.

"The way," observed Manecão gloomily, "in which I frighten the Senhora Dona!"

The teeth of the girl chattered with emotion and she trembled in all her limbs.

The Mineiro impatiently strode towards her and seized her by an arm.

"But you have no fever?" he cried. "What is this, girl?" Then half smiling, he turned towards Manecão: "I know what it is. She is startled—on—on seeing you so suddenly. Come, come, 'Nocencia, leave off trembling. Immediately, I say."

"I wish to—to return to my room," she murmured, and, reaching her hand to the wall, with tottering steps she slowly retired to her chamber.

The muleteer assumed a sullen, downcast expression, and from under his knitted brows he followed with his gaze the retreating form of she whom he already considered his wife.

Pereira, with his arms akimbo, placed himself in front of the tropeiro.[45]

---

[45] A muleteer.

CHAPTER XXVII: HUNTING THE DOE.

"What do you think of that now?" said he, with an air of surprise. "No one can count upon women, eh?"

Manecão made no reply.

At last he suddenly observed, in a very drawling tone, and pausing at every word, "Your—daughter—has—seen—some one."

The Mineiro flushed, and, almost stuttering, replied, "No, no —that is, she saw—but there, every day, you know—she—she sees people. Why do you ask me this?"

"For nothing."

"Now explain yourself. You thus ask me A question that makes me a—a little confused. This is a serious business. I gave you my word of honour that my daughter shall be your wife. The town already knows it, and—and with me, I want no stories. That is what I say."

Manecão looked up suddenly.

"It is well," said he. "Let us be slow, careful, and sure, for thus I have been all my life. I will return soon, but now I will see after my horse."

He went away, leaving Pereira a prey to the most conflicting suppositions.

Days passed by without the two men once touching upon the subject that grieved their hearts. Both, calm in appearance, lived a common life. They went together to the plantations, they took their meals together, they hunted together, and only separated at the hour of repose; for then the Mineiro went to his room at the rear, and Manecão occupied the guests' room in the front.

Innccencia did not appear. She scarcely left her chamber, alleging, as an excuse, that she had a return of the ague; but although her body was not affected, her mind was tortured with her passion and despair, and bitter tears, especially at night, inundated her face.

"Meu Deus!" she wailed. "What will become of me? Nossa Senhora da Guia succour me. What can I do, I, a poor unhappy girl of the Sertão?"

On her knees, before the rudely-fashioned oratory, illumined by coarse candles, she prayed with fervour, murmuring the formula she was accustomed to recite before retiring to rest.

Suddenly she hesitated. "I would that I knew a prayer that would better ease my heart, that would relieve me in my misery to-day." And, as if carried away by some inspiration, she prostrated herself, murmuring, "My Lady, mother of the Virgin who never sinned, oh! I pray thee go unto God and ask him to have pity on me. Not to leave me thus with this pain here within me. Extend your hand over me, but if it is a crime to love Cyrino, then I pray thee send me death."

At times, Innocencia experienced in herself the elements of resistance, for she had inherited something of the character of her father, some of his strong and obstinate disposition.

"I will go," she cried, with flaming eyes, "to the church, and in the face of the padre I will cry, No! no! Kill me! But I will not marry that man."

When some vivid memory of Cyrino crossed her mind she was almost beside herself with despair. Her passion filled her breast with fire "What is this, meu Deus? Has that man put the evil eye upon me. But, oh, Cyrino! Cyrino! Come back! Come back! Come and take me! Oh! I shall die!" She fell upon

CHAPTER XXVII: HUNTING THE DOE.

her couch shivering with nervous excitement.

One day, Pereira suddenly entered her room and found her bedewed with tears.

"What has troubled you, my child, the last few days?" he inquired, in a tender tone of voice. He was outwardly calm, but his expression was that of decision.

Innocencia shrunk within herself, like a dove that feels a rude hand is about to grasp it.

The father gently drew her towards him and laid her head upon his breast. "Come, 'Nocencia. Tell me, what is it all? You shut yourself in your room, and Manecão is there outside asking for you constantly. This is not pretty. Is he, or is he not, your bridegroom?"

The girl's tears poured afresh.

"A woman certainly should not throw herself in the face of any man," observed her father "but it is also not right to be peevish like this. It is sickening!—a husband as he all but is."

Suddenly, Innocencia ceased weeping, and, withdrawing herself from her father's arms, she stood rigidly in front of him, and, with the fire of resolution flashing from her eyes, she said:

"Father, would you know what all this means?,"

"Yes."

"It is because I—I ought not——"

"Ought not what?"

"To marry."

At these words Pereira stared at her with astonishment, and

his jaw fell with the shock of surprise.

"What?" he almost screamed.

The girl comprehended that the struggle was about to commence, and, summoning all her courge, she replied with apparent calmness:

"Yes, my father, this marriage ought not to take place."

"Are you crazy?" observed Pereira, with assumed tranquillity.

Innocencia, with her cheeks burning with flushes, proceeded to say very rapidly:

"Father, I will tell you all. Do not wish me ill. It was but a dream, it is true. The other day, before this man arrived, I was sleeping, and I had a dream. In this dream—do you hear, father?—my mother came descending from Heaven. Poor mother! She was so white that it made me sad. But she was dressed so beautifully, with a dress all blue."

"Your mother?" interrupted Pereira, with a slight emotion.

"Sim, Senhor, she herself."

"But how could you know her? She died when you were a baby."

"All the same," continued Innocencia, "I knew at once that it was my mother. She looked at me—oh, so lovingly!—and asked me, 'Where is your father?' I answered tremblingly, 'He is in the fields, would you wish him to come here?' 'No,' she said to me. 'It is not necessary. Tell him that I came here to prevent Manecão marrying you, or otherwise you will be most unhappy.'"

"And afterwards?" inquired Pereira, raising his head with a sombre air and wildly rolling his eyes.

CHAPTER XXVII: HUNTING THE DOE.

"Afterwards, she said more. 'If this man marries you a great misfortune will happen in — in this house' and then, without any more words, she disappeared."

"Pereira fixed a keen, inquiring gaze upon his daughter, while a suspicion flashed across his mind.

"What marks had your mother on her face?"

Innocencia suddenly became deadly pale, and raising both hands to her head and uttering a wailing cry, she exclaimed:

"I know not — I — I am lying. It is all a story. It is a lie — I saw not my mother. Oh! mother! mother! forgive me." And throwing herself full length upon the couch, and her scattered rich raven tresses shrouding her gleaming white shoulders, she remained immovable.

Pereira silently contemplated her for a long, long time, knowing not what to think nor what to say. Presently, as if seized with some sudden resolve, he leant over the figure of the girl and murmured, or rather hoarsely hissed in her ear:

"'Nocencia, in a little while Manecão will return from the fields. You shall go to him, and if you wear not a kind face — I — I will kill you!" And raising his voice he added, "Do you hear? I will kill you! Rather would I see you dead than — than the house of a Mineiro dishonoured."

He then rushed from the apartment, leaving Innocencia in the same position.

"Very well!" she muttered, "it is but what I want, then I die."

CHAPTER XXVIII: IN THE HOUSE OF CESARIO.

Cyrino's first endeavours as soon as he was established in the house of his new host were to create a good impression. He attended to the ailments of a sick slave, he made the most of his acquaintance and friendship with Pereira, he conversed repeatedly about him, and, incidentally, mentioned Innocencia.

Antonio Cesario then inquired, "Has Mecê seen her?"

"Certainly," replied the youth. "The truth is I cured her of ague."

"Ah! She is quite a belle, I believe."

"So she seems to be."

"That is, I say so, because anyhow in a few days from now she marries. Don't you know that?"

"So I have heard."

"Well, it is the truth. The bridegroom passed through here and carried with him my consent. He is a well-to-do man. The little one ought to be contented. Ah! not everybody in the Sertão is so fortunate. They have the bad habit about here of blindly arranging marriages, and sometimes a lusty young fellow gets entangled with some old screw, or a pretty girl finds herself bound to some wrinkled old fellow. Cruz! Once the blessed word is given, it is a bond that cannot be broken. It is all over, whether for better or for worse."

Cyrino found the occasion propitious, and replied with some vivacity, "Well, are these ideas not yours also?"

CHAPTER XXVIII: IN THE HOUSE OF CESARIO.

"It depends," responded Cesario cautiously. "It is the parents who have to examine into these matters."

"Without doubt. But suppose—suppose, for example—that your goddaughter did not like Manecão."

"If she did not like him?"

"Yes."

"What does that matter? A girl like her knows not what is good or bad for her. No one would think of consulting her. Women! What they desire is to get married. They draw the line only at carrapatos,[46] because you can't tell which are the males." He laughed boisterously at his concluding assertion; then suddenly resuming a serious expression, he asked, "Why are we thus chattering on this subject? I am no friend of such things. It seems to be that Mecê is a bit of a nomorato himself."

"I?" protested Cyrino quickly.

"Without doubt. I never talk about such things. Woman is made to live close to her loom, to attend her children, and bring them up in the fear of God. She is not made for a man to converse with, not even to speak about."

Thus the same ideas predominated in the mind of Cesario as in Pereira's, the same gross contempt for the weak sex, the same readiness to suspect any one individual or to transform the meaning of any careless word dropped in their suspicious hearing. "My goddaughter," continued Cesario, "ought to raise her hands to heaven. She has found a husband who will make her happy and the mother of a good round dozen of children."

Cyrino trembled, but said nothing. Everywhere, fresh

---

[46]Carrapatos are a species of ticks which mainly infest the pastoral regions.

obstacles continually arose against him that apparently nothing could surmount. Finally, he decided to seize the bull by the horns. At the worst, he would only receive a rebuff, and in a desperate game he would hazard yet a daring throw.

"Senhor Cesario," said he on the following morning, "I want very much to speak with yon in private."

"With me?"

"Sim, Senhor."

"Well, I am here at your orders."

"I would like to go outside, for what I would say to you no one can—no one ought to hear."

"Wah! You frighten me. Then have you secrets to tell me?"

"I have."

"Well, then, we will talk outside as you wish. At midday meet me in my plantation. Do you know where it is?"

"I know."

"Wait for me by the fallen withered peroba-tree."

"I will be there."

Long before the indicated hour, Cyrino, consumed with impatience, was at the try sting-place. Resolved to relate to this man, without reserve, the story of his love, to unbosom himself to one whom he barely knew and who had no reasons for sympathising with him, and on whom, above all things, depended His happiness, Cyrino considered those moments the decisive ones of his life.

Under these circumstances the mind sees in all its surroundings omens of good or evil portent; and, on this

CHAPTER XXVIII: IN THE HOUSE OF CESARIO.

occasion, all nature seemed to Cyrino to wear a gloomy aspect. Although it did not rain, the sky was heavily overcast with clouds. The heavens were leaden coloured; and away to the west masses of dark clouds denoted thunder in the coming afternoon. The locality was also a dreary one. Over a huge area, covered with the pale green verdure of sugar cane, with clusters of flowering tops showing the approach to maturity — here and there arose, in weird grandeur, the massive trunks and leafless branches of colossal trees. Some, from base to topmost boughs, were charcoaled with the past fires of the bush burning previous to seed time; others had lost their foliage in consequence of the deep circumferential incision of the axe, which had impeded the ascension of the sap. These still struggled for life, as was seen in the withered sprouts of the topmost branches.

When the day is bright, these scattered giants of the forest — which through the robustness of their hearts had resisted the flames or the force of man — served as perches for innumerable flocks of parrots, perriquitos, love-birds, and macaws, which raise a concert enough to deaden an echo. On this occasion, however, all was silent. Only now and then were heard the blows of the red-crested woodpecker, which, rapidly ascending the trunks by a zig-zag route, explored every worm-eaten crevice and cranny.

Antonio Cesario arrived at the appointed hour. For protection against any stray jaguar or other wild animal he carried a gun in his arms. His usually placid face showed more disturbance than mere curiosity explained.

"Here I am, doctor," said he, resting the weapon against the charred stump of a tree and seating himself close to Cyrino. "I am ready to listen to you just as long as you please."

Cyrino had long thought of the approach of this moment, yet now he could find no way to broach his declarations. He had mused continually upon a thousand pretexts, but upon nothing had he resolved.

It was therefore almost stuttering that he responded:

"The Senhor, me—that is—I hope you will excuse the—the inconvenience that—that I give you—I——"

"No, it is no inconvenience at all."

"But you must be—er—surprised at what I asked—to—to come and speak with me—in a solitary place—with one who is only a guest, such as any other, such as the many your open house receives every day——"

"Well, really——"

"However, in a short time all will he clear and explained, but if, after I have spoken—I—I offend you, I crave your pardon beforehand, do you hear? Senhor Cesario," continued Cyrino, after a brief pause, "if you saw a man hurrying down a cataract to destruction and you could throw him a rope and save him, would you not do so?"

"Certainly I would," replied the other, with animation. "Even at the risk of my own life I would refuse help to no man, be he rich or poor, white or black, free man or slave."

"Well then," exclaimed Cyrino precipitately, "I am just such a man, in peril of my life, and who will be lost unless you, and only you, will save me." Repressing the reply of his listener he continued: "Do not think that I am mad. No. I am as sound in my mind as you are, and I tell you only the absolute truth. One word will explain all. I die of passion for a woman, and that woman is—is—is your goddaughter—Innocencia!"

CHAPTER XXVIII: IN THE HOUSE OF CESARIO.

Cesario sprang to his feet in one bound. His lips trembled, his eyes suddenly became bloodshot, and his hand reached for the weapon by his side. "What is that you say?" he gasped, as he fixed Ms gaze on Cyrino, who, divining his thoughts, also rose to his feet, and placing himself face to face with Cesario exclaimed:

"Kill me!" he cried. "Kill me! Aye, it would be but a favour to me to put an end to this wretched life."

The other, already repenting of the gesture he had made, and somewhat vexed at his hastiness, replied sullenly:

"I have no cause to kill you, you never did me any harm."

"No," proceeded Cyrino a little unreasonably, "I ask you this; if you have any charity, if you are good, if you love your children, if you have a mother in Heaven—for all that, on my knees I beg you to kill me! kill me!"

And falling on his knees at the feet of Cesario, he buried his face in his hands.

The Mineiro contemplated him for some time in great surprise. Presently his countenance softened, and stooping over the young man, he patted him kindly on the shoulder and gently said:

"What story is this, doctor? This is madness! Tell me what it all means. I want to know all the ins and outs of your story. I am a man of the Sertão, a Mineiro of the law, but I know how to treat people properly."

On hearing these words Cyrino recovered some animation, and, rising to his feet, he seated himself by the side of Cesario and straightway told him everything—the despair that possessed him, the certainty that he had won the love of Innocencia, and the implacable sentence of Pereira.

Cesario listened to him with attention. Only now and then he gravely shook his head and allowed this exclamation to escape him:

"Ah! women, women!"

After Cyrino had finished speaking, his auditor gazed fixedly at him, and, with a severe expression, he asked:

"Now tell me the truth, doctor. Have you never exchanged words with Innocencia? Never been alone with her?"

"I have," the other somewhat nervously replied.

A rush of blood tinged scarlet the face of Cesario. "Then," he retorted, the disgrace— —"

"Meu Deus!" cried Cyrino with enthusiasm. "May the soul of my mother descend to inferno if Innocencia is not as pure as — —"

Cesario repressed the exclamation with a gesture. "Enough, young man," he gravely said, "who swears thus does not lie. I also, in my time, endured an unhappy passion, and know what it is to suffer."

CHAPTER XXVIII: IN THE HOUSE OF CESARIO.

"Oh, Senhor Cesario, save me!"

"What can I do? Do you not know that, now, she does not even belong to her father, her own father? She belongs to the word of honour, and the word of a Mineiro is never recalled. Did you not know that when you allowed love to enter by your eyes? Do not speak about her. Women do not think. What women want is to see men grovelling on their knees after them; they will sacrifice everything to obtain their whims, and for a mere amorous intrigue in the street—piff—away goes the honour of their homes in a second."

"No," protested Cyrino, "she is not so."

"Then is she better than other women?" inquired Cesario disdainfully.

"Ay, that she is, better than all in this world. Above her is only Nossa Senhora!"

The enthusiasm with which these words were uttered brought a smile to the face of the Mineiro.

"Rubbish!" said he. "Well said some one when he declared that love is a lunacy. It makes a man a misery, and ——"

"And then?" interrupted Cyrino.

"Then what? Have I not already told you enough? My goddaughter belongs to Manecão just as if she were a pistol or a silver-mounted drinking-horn which Pereira had presented to him. There are no means whatever of regaining her."

The youth, however, was not disheartened. For a long time he spoke with true eloquence, appealing principally to the protection which is due from those who carry a child to the baptismal font, to one's second child, to the little pagan for whom the godparent becomes responsible before God.[47]

Thus striking home through the religious sentiments, he considerably affected the feelings of the Mineiro.

"Speak not to me thus," said the latter, for you only want to make me take your views. Who knows, moreover, that Innocencia cares for you? Who, I say?"

"Your own heart whispers it to you," Cyrino calmly replied. "You, a man of honour, do you believe I am lying? That all I say is false? Tell me, do you think so?"

Cesario murmured, "Well, let us suppose it is true, but— —"

"Ah!" cried the youth enthusiastically. "You feel that your heart tells you that your own goddaughter is abandoned to her fate—that she will be sacrificed—and now—ah! You stop your ears, crying, 'I do not want to hear, I do not want to fulfil my sacred promise!' Why then did the Senhor give his word of honour about which you think so much? May Nossa Senhora protect her and deliver her from this world. Ah! surely this will weigh heavily on your conscience. And when, some day, you hear that Innocencia has died of a broken heart, you will then think to yourself that you lent a hand to dig her grave."

Cesario was considerably moved by this appeal, and it was with unfeigned anxiety that he retorted, "What stories are these you tell me? I, in my home, hitherto living so peacefully and interfering with no one, and now, here I am, mixed up with all this trouble and mischief! Who sent you here?"

"Who should it be," retorted Cyrino, "but Innocencia? I barely knew you; once only I saw you. No, it was that angel who said

---

[47]In Brazil the obligations of a godparent to his or her godchild are, by custom, of a very serious and binding character, and especially include the duty of guarding the material welfare and general interests of the godchild.—[Transl.]

CHAPTER XXVIII: IN THE HOUSE OF CESARIO.

to me, 'Go and appeal to my godfather, it is the last resource, for if he does not protect me, then—then indeed we are lost for ever.'"

These words finally convinced Cesario. He remained a while silently meditating, Cyrino watching him with breathless anxiety.

"Very well," the Mineiro at last observed, in a grave and hesitating tone. "I shall have to think over all that you have told me."

"Oh, Senhor Cesario!"

"I will take two days to think the matter over, for once I make up my mind there's an end of it. At the end of that time I will mount my horse and ride over to Pereira's house."

"Yes, yes," murmured the young man.

"To-morrow, at daybreak, you must leave here and go and wait for me in Sant'Anna."

"I will go! I am saved!"

Cesario paused a moment and then said:

"Listen, I now want you to swear an oath by the ashes of your mother."

"I am ready."

"By the salvation of your soul."

"By the salvation of my soul," repeated Cyrino.

"By the eternal life."

Cyrino bowed his head.

"Swear!"

The youth crossed his two forefingers and kissed them with unction, at the same time drooping his eyes and turning pale.

"You take an oath before you know what it is for," said Cesario. "That gives one a good idea of your character. I will do everything to help you, but I impose one condition. If you are ready to accept it, your oath remains good, if not—then it becomes invalid."

"Meu Deus! What may it be?" murmured Cyrino.

"That you remain waiting for me in Sant'Anna. If I appear there within eight days we will go together to the house of Pereira. If not, it will be a sign that I shall not kelp you; in that case, you will return here and wait for your baggage, which I will send to fetch. It shall then be understood that, never more, never more will you seek to put eyes on Innocencia — neither even speak of her, nor mention her name. Do you accept?"

"I accept," responded the young man with exultation, "But remain certain of one thing; if the Senhor does not arrive in the town by the appointed time, you may pray for the soul of Cyrino, for then he will surely have left this world of afflictions."

Cesario sadly shook his head, and went away without uttering another word.

CHAPTER XXIX: THE DOE AT BAY.

We left Innocencia as weak in body as she was resolute in mind. She foresaw what trials and difficulties she would have to undergo, and strengthened her resolves by continual meditations upon her unhappiness.

She was on her knees before an image of Nossa Senhora, when, from the adjoining room, the voice of her father caused her to arise.

"'Nocencia!" he called.

The poor girl passed her hand rapidly over her face to remove the vestiges of her copious weeping, and with an almost firm step she proceeded towards the room.

Pereira and Manecão were seated close to the table. The little dwarf Tico, seated on the doorstep and basking in the pallid rays of a partly cloud-obscured sun, was playing, or pretended to play, with some young ducks.

"I am here, my father," said Innocencia, in a clear but slightly tremulous voice.

Manecão gazed at her with an air half sullen, half eager with passion, and feeling that he was called upon to say something, he observed:

"At last, then, the Dona has come out of her nest, eh? Is it to find some sunshine? Is that it, eh?"

The girl made no reply, but gazed at him so calmly and with such insistance that he was forced to lower his eyes.

"She has been ill, you know," apologised Pereira. And turning to his daughter, he continued: "Sit yourself down here close to us. Manecão wants to talk to you about something particular."

"Ha! ha! She knows what it is," laughingly observed the muleteer, endeavouring to be jocular.

"I do not know," Innocencia replied, in calm, incisive tones.

"She is—ah!—trying to be funny," muttered Manecão. "Well then—have you already forgotten—what—what I arranged with your father?"

With the same calm intonation she replied, "I do not remember."

Some moments of silence followed.

A storm of anger was rapidly accumulating in the breast of Pereira, and his frowning eyes glanced, now at Manecão, now at the courageous daughter.

"Well," said he suddenly, "if you do not remember, I, here, am not so forgetful."

"Now," recommenced Manecão, as he rose from his seat and moved so as to be nearer to the girl, "she is only pretending to be ill. Our marriage— —"

"Your marriage?" inquired Innocencia, in assumed surprise.

"Yes."

"But with whom?"

"Wah!" exclaimed Manecão, utterly dumbfounded. "Who else but you?"

Pereira turned livid with rage. The little dwarf watched the scene with rapt attention. His twinkling eyes scintillated like black diamonds, and his limbs trembled with impatience.

CHAPTER XXIX: THE DOE AT BAY.

At the reply of Manecão Innocencia arose, and, moving swiftly away as if to seek a refuge behind a chair, she exclaimed, "I? I marry the Senhor? Never! Rather would I welcome death. Never! Never can it be."

Manecão shivered as if struck by a blow.

Pereira tried to spring to his feet, but for some instants he seemed absolutely paralysed.

"You are mad!" he stammered. "You are mad!" And, fiercely clutching at the table, he arose, terrible in his wrath. "Then will you not marry him?" he thundered, his very teeth chattering with passion.

"No," cried the girl desperately. "Rather would I— —"

She could not finish, for Pereira grasped her hand with such violence that he almost forced her to fall upon her knees; and then, with his utmost strength, he flung her away from him, hurling her against the wall, where she sank heavily to the ground.

As the unhappy girl fell she uttered a low moaning cry of pain, and, stretched on the floor, she grasped her breast with both hands. Her face turned deadly pale, and from a slight wound on her brow slowly oozed a few drops of blood.

In the madness of his rage it seemed as though Pereira would throw himself upon her and trample out her life with his feet, but, stopping suddenly, he raised his hands to his face to hide the tears which welled from his eyes.

During the whole sad scene Manecão made not the least gesture. He grimly noted everything, his physiognomy was impassive and unmoved as marble itself; but in his breast raged a very volcano.

A lugubrious silence reigned for some time in the room.

The dwarf approached Innocencia, and, taking her hand, assisted her to rise to a sitting posture. Then, amidst many caresses, he showed her by signs the necessity of retiring.

Only by a great effort could Innocencia follow that advice and, with halting steps and trembling limbs, and assisted by Tico, she went away from the presence of her persecutors.

Neither of the two men made the slightest attempt to detain her. Side by side, silent and passive, both seemed utterly demoralised by the magnitude of their imagined disgrace.

Manecã, his jaws clenched and his eyes fiercely flashing under his lowered brows, passed a hand rapidly and continuously over his huge moustache. Pereira, with his head sunk upon his breast, seemed a picture of despair. At last he said:

"I must draw this charge I have within me or I shall go mad. Well, whoever may be the man, Manecão, 'Nocencia, at least, is now lost to us, for some one must have put the evil eye upon her."

"Who is that man?" growled Manecão, in a harsh and threatening tone.

"Now I see it all. I, even I, received the 'diabo' himself in my house. I was watchful, but the seed of evil had already taken root."

"But who is he?" Manecão again impatiently inquired.

"A rascal! An infamous fellow! A foreigner who stopped here and robbed me of the peace that Deus blessed me with."

Pereira then hastily related all the attempts of the German Meyer, attempts which had been discovered, but which,

CHAPTER XXIX: THE DOE AT BAY.

unhappily (at least so he, Pereira, supposed), had produced their fatal fruits. "Ah!" said he finally, and lowering his voice, "that cur thought only of cajoling women, and then, with a kick, to leave them in the dust. To-morrow I will be after him and— —"

"What for?" interrupted Manecão.

"The vultures shall answer you."

"To kill him?"

"Yes."

After a short pause the muleteer said:

"It shall not be you who is to give an account of his skin."

"Why not?"

"Because this is a business that belongs to me. The Senhor is the father it is true, but I am the bridegroom. He has played the fool with us both, but any way the German shall bite the dust."

"Well, so be it," concorded Pereira. "Start to-morrow or to-day, ay, this instant if it be possible. Such a cursed cur should be killed at once, as you would kill a mad dog. Go quickly, and return to tell me that the man no longer exists. As an old man, as a father, I will bless the hand that kills him. Upon these, my white hairs, let the blood fall."

All this conversation had been listened to by some one else, the dwarf Tico. Little by little, and with his eyes sparkling with excitement, he had gradually approached the table. Suddenly he placed himself between the two men.

"What do you want here?" the Mineiro roughly inquired.

The little man immediately commenced to demonstrate, by

careful and very expressive gestures, that he was cognisant of all the projects and that he participated in the same sentiment of indignation and desperation that afflicted the owner of the house. Then, quickening his gesticulations, by some half-inarticulate sounds, he showed Pereira that he was labouring under a misapprehension in regard to some person, and with great skill and a perfect mimicry—now raising his arm to indicate a height, now with a movement of his hands to describe the physiognomy—he indicated so clearly the characteristics of Meyer and Cyrino that Pereira at once recognised them, and observed:

"I see, I see, Tico, you want to speak of the doctor, and—and the other."

Here the dwarf made an impatient gesture of negation, and, pointing towards the chamber of Innocencia, he made his auditors understand that the German had nothing to do with that region.

The two men were startled.

"Then," stammered Pereira"then who can it be? Meu Deus, not Cyrino?"

"Yes—yes," articulated the dwarf excitedly, and impatiently nodding his head.

"The doctor?" protested Pereira. "Nonsense!"

Tico with great ability demonstrated his proofs. He gesticulated like one possessed. He ran out of the house; denounced the interviews; imitated the night wanderings of Cyrino; showed the place in the orange-grove where he saw all that passed and the branches broken by his fall; he repeated the mysterious cry that had provoked the shot at daybreak; finally, he explained by such expressive signs and

CHAPTER XXIX: THE DOE AT BAY.

such movements of bis bead and physiognomy, that any remaining doubts disappeared at once from the mind of Pereira.

Now that all the previous mystery was so clearly unravelled, it came with so startling a shock to Pereira, that be gasped for breath in the paroxysm of his anger. He staggered like a drunken man, he reeled, his eyes became bloodshot, and he had to grasp the table for support.

"Ha! scoundrel!" be gasped, and became purple with excitement and rage. "Thou shalt pay me. Ah! scoundrel! villain!" and turning to Manecão be added, "Give me this—he is mine."

The muleteer calmly shook his head. "No," he replied, in a low harsh voice. "He belongs to me. He humbugged you and made a fool of me."

"Then," exclaimed Pereira hastily, "depart today! Go at once! Instantly! And when you return say only, 'We are revenged,' and Innocencia shall be yours." After pausing a moment with considerable irritation be concluded, "If she will accept you."

"That we shall have to talk about."

The Mineiro uttered a cry of despair. "Meu Deus!" he exclaimed, in seeming agony. "In what a world we live! A man who enters my home, who eats of what I eat, who sleeps beneath my roof tree, who drinks water from my stream, this man arrives here, and, of an abode of peace and honour, he makes it a place of turmoil and shame! No! May a thousand lightnings blast me if this miserable being any longer breathes the air that surrounds me. No, no! A thousand times no! And clear out at once the canalha he brought here, sons of inferno like their master. I will spit on their faces. Away with them like curs as they are! Thieves! Assasins! I— —"

Manecão calmly interrupted him by saying:

"Do nothing, no one must know what is passing here. No one. Do you understand?

"And then?"

"Make out that you have received a letter from Sant'Anna, and that the owl wants his men to wait for him at Leal's. Do you hear?"

Pereira made signs that he comprehended all.

"Afterwards," added Manecão, in a sinister voice, "hands to the work."

"You say well," retorted Pereira, "but have patience with me, my head is all in a hurly-burly, and throbbing and singing as if it would split. Well, show that you are now the owner of this house and do what you please. I deliver myself to you bound hand and foot. Everything here belongs to you. While the honour of a Mineiro is not redeemed I will not raise my head. Meu Deus! meu Deus! What a disgrace!"

"Courage, courage," interrupted Manecão. "If revenge fails to hide my miseries I will move to the regions of the Apa. Ah! I feel about to die, my head seems full of fire. Ah me!" and utterly prostrated by his emotions he stretched his arms upon the table and on them bowed his troubled head.

Manecão gently tapped his shoulder.

"What is this, my father?" said he. "Be a man, or what serves it? Look at your misfortune, which is mine also, manfully, as you would at the rascal, face to face. Are you not consoled at the certainty that that man will soon— —"

CHAPTER XXIX: THE DOE AT BAY.

"Ah, yes!" replied Pereira, raising his head; and observing that the dwarf had gone away, he added, "But what shall we do with that morsel of humanity who knows everything?"

"Do not let him leave the house."

"Manecão, he is like a flash, in an instant, and before one knows, he turns up in Sucuriu or even in the Corredor."

"Very well, then he must learn that—that only a wink of his eyes, when it is not wanted, may cost him dear, very dear. Umph."

"At least," implored Pereira, "go at once and clear those fellows out my barn—go. If I could sleep a little—I might forget somewhat; but—all me!"

With these words the Mineiro slowly left the room for his own quarters.

Manecão promptly despatched the attendants of Cyrino, who soon afterwards were on their way to the house of Leal.

Then the Sertanejo mounted his horse, and, spurring the animal to its utmost speed, he dashed away towards Sant'Anna da Paranahyba, which he reached when the night was far advanced.

CHAPTER XXX: TOO LATE.

During two whole days, Manecão followed the trail of Cyrino, and as unerringly as would a sleuth-hound, and by means of the habitual caution engendered by the habits of his wandering life, he succeeded in tracking his victim, step by step, without being once observed. Thus he noted that his rival, mounted on his mule, had proceeded to a certain point of the road, and there had waited as if he expected some one to arrive, but who failed to appear. On going, Cyrino showed impatience and uneasiness; on returning, he seemed melancholy, distraught with care, and absorbed in profound meditation.

The unhappy youth had indeed gone to the trysting-place of Cesario, in the vain hopes that possibly he might come before the appointed time. That time, however, had now nearly expired and the hour for the abandonment of all hope or the consummation of his happiness was on the eve of its approach. Ah! if, with the powers of Joshua, he could but stay the march of the sun until his Saviour resolved to extend to him the hand of help.

And now the week was ending. If Cesario appeared not at the finish of the hours, then would commence to reign the oath he swore, that irrevocable oath.

"I shall destroy myself," said Cyrino; "they will then at least know that I keep my word."

With this resolution the youth again left the town, traversed the Rio Paranahyba, and, as before followed the road of S. Francisco de Salles for about twelve miles.

The day was clear, most beautiful. From all around sounded

CHAPTER XXX: TOO LATE.

the songs of birds. Amidst the bush, the cicadas bah'd and whistled and whirred, and on the green sward the partridges plaintively cried. Cyrino was extremely agitated, and heard nothing of surrounding sounds. His fixed gaze was never removed from the road ahead in the anxious watch for any signs of the bearer of good tidings.

Suddenly, there fell upon his ear the sounds of some one approaching, the sounds of a galloping horse. His heart beat so violently that it seemed to be in a gallop itself. But alas! the sound came from behind him. Doubtless some one from the town. Cyrino continued his march.

The rapid clatter of hoofs indicated some horseman riding at full speedy and soon it would be seen who was thus riding so furiously in the torrid heat of the day. The youth, however, heeded not, so much so, that he barely glanced at the horseman who passed him by in bounding strides and almost dashed against Cyrino's animal. Immediately afterwards he heard also the sounds of some horseman coming from the opposite direction, while the rider who had just passed seemed to have halted a little further on. Cyrino now awoke from his lethargy, and, vigorously spurring his animal, presently found himself face to face with—Manecão. Instinctively he turned pale, and his rival also changed colour.

Both men reined in their animals, and intently gazed at one another for some seconds, one in suspicion and astonishment, the other with ill-concealed fury.

"What are you doing here?" inquired the muleteer, in a tone of provocation.

"I?"

"Yes, you."

"That is good. See you not that I am on a journey?"

"Ah! A journey? Humph! On the prowl, eh?"

"On the prowl? No, I am no brute beast," replied Cyrino warmly, at the same time raising the cover of his pistol-holster.

"Then if you are not a prowler, what are you then?"

"I am what I am, and that does not concern you."

The face of Manecão became distorted with rage, and, in one bound, he brought his horse alongside Cyrino's, when, in a low harsh voice, he exclaimed:

"I will tell you then what you are. You are a thief! a very cur!"

At this insult Cyrino drew out his pistol.

"I will shoot you," he cried excitedly, "if you continue to thus annoy me."

The muleteer smiled contemptuously. "Ho! ho!" he jeered. "How brave we are! We can actually handle a pistol."

"Let us finish this!" cried Cyrino.

"Let us," retorted Manecão, with seeming calmness.

"But who are you?" asked Cyrino.

"I?"

"Yes, you?"

"Then do you not know me?"

"No—no," stammered Cyrino.

"Do you know 'Nocencia, then?" thundered Manecão in the loudest tones of his powerful voice; and instantly drawing a

CHAPTER XXX: TOO LATE.

long horse pistol from his belt he discharged its contents full at the breast of Cyrino, who immediately fell to the earth.

Two fierce cries rent the air; one, a wail of agony, the other, a yell of triumph.

Cyrino, face downwards, was stretched full length on the ground, and, although blood was oozing from his mouth, with a great effort he raised his head to confront his implacable foe, who gazed impassively at his victim.

Cyrino broke into loud vociferations: "Assassin! Villain!—Ah! Yes!—Yes!—I do know Innocencia!—She is mine!—Scoundrel! You—you have killed me—but thou hast killed her also. What have I done to thee? Deus will curse thee—yes, ah men Deus! meus Santos!—Curses upon this assassin. Fly!—Hide thyself where thou wilt, but my shade shall ever follow thee."

"So much the better," calmly observed Manecão from the height of his saddle, "that is just what I would like."

"Ah! you would?" continued Cyrino, in a very hoarse voice. "Then so be it! By day and by night—my shade—shall—shall be with thee always—for—for ever."

He ceased for a few moments in a paroxysm of pain, and writhed on the ground with the agony of his wound. He passed a hand across his brow, already damp with the cold and clammy dews of death. Gradually, as his respiration became more laboured, the wild expression of his face changed to one more soft and gentle.

"No," said he gravely and in a tone of resignation, "I must not die—thus—I must leave this world as a Christian—I must forgive thee—Manecão, I do forgive thee—for—for the sake of Christo—who died—on the Cross. I—I forgive thee, Manecão—Nosso Senhor, have pity on me—but I forgive thee—

Manecão, do you hear?"

The piteous manner in which the dying man uttered these sentences sensibly affected Manecão, and caused him to glare at his victim with startled eyes of horror, while his frame trembled with agitation. As if with considerable effort, he hoarsely muttered:

"I want not your forgiveness."

"No matter," gently responded Cyrino. "It is—it is given from my heart. Take it, and welcome it. Ah! poor Innocencia! Who knows if—if she will not follow me soon? Ah! this agony! Oh, Manecão! Give me water—water for the love of Deus. Man, get off your horse. It is a dying man who asks." With extended arms and appealing looks, for a few moments he pitifully entreated Manecão, and then raising himself to a sitting posture, he almost screamed, "Water—water—give me water—and I will bless thee!"

The muleteer felt huge drops of perspiration trickle down his brow. He wanted to fly, but horror held him captive. It seemed as if his glaring eyes followed, step by step, the agonies of his victim. That scene appeared to him as a nightmare, and a complete torpor deadened his limbs and faculties. What aroused him from such a state of trance were the patter of hoofs upon the sandy road.

Cyrino also heard them, and wistfully and anxiously his. eyes glanced in the direction of the sound, while a smile of bitter melancholy stole over his face.

Manecão, now thoroughly aroused, immediately clapped spurs to his horse, and, in the twinkling of an eye, disappeared in a cloud of dust.

At the same moment, in the opposite direction and rounding a

CHAPTER XXX: TOO LATE.

bend of the road, a horseman appeared. Antonio Cesario himself.

On seeing a man stretched on the ground, he hastened his movements. "The doctor!" he exclaimed, horrified at the sight, and hastily dismounting.

"Even I," replied Cyrino, in a faint voice.

"But, Santo Deus!" cried the Mineiro, "who has done thee this foul deed?" and hurrying towards the young man, he knelt by his side and raised the body on his knee. "Who was the assassin?"

"No one," murmured the miserable youth. "It was—destiny—I die content. Give me—water—water—and speak to me of—of Innocencia."

"Water, my poor fellow!" exclaimed Cesario, in despair. "Here in the midst of the bush? Why the nearest stream is, at least, twelve miles away."

"Ah!" replied Cyrino wearily. "If there is none to quench the—the thirst of the body—stay the—cravings of my soul. Innocencia? Where is she? Let me see her. Ah! tell her I died for her—for her sake."

"But tell me, who is the assassin?" anxiously inquired the Mineiro.

"It is not worth—mentioning," responded Cyrino, in the intervals of his rigours. "Think only of—of—me. Now—listen—I never did ill to—to any one—I have no—no great sins to—to answer for. Think you that—that Deus will forgive me?"

"I do indeed," earnestly responded Cesario.

"What have I done in—in my life? Perhaps—deceived my—

my fellows in saying I—I was a medico. But many have—have I cured. Nothing—else—do I—remember——"

The shades of death came stealing over the face of Cyrino. The light of life departed from his glazing eyes, his jaw drooped, his nostrils dilated, and a sinister pallor heightened, by contrast, the dark shades of his hair and beard.

Cesario seated himself on the ground in order to give an easier support to the body of the dying man, and two huge tears rolled down his sunburnt cheeks.

A slight shiver agitated the body of Cyrino. "Now," he murmured, in a still low voice—"my day—has arrived. But—I ask—thee—say nothing; your goddaughter—do not allow—her—to—to marry—Manecão."

"Then," quickly interrupted Cesario, "it was then he who ——?"

"No—no—but she—will be—unhappy. Do you hear? Oh! promise me."

"I do promise you, my poor fellow," sternly replied Cesario, "I will even swear to——"

"Good—good," whispered Cyrino, as he heaved a sigh of content. Now—welcome—death. The Saints of Paradise—take me—and call for—for—"With a final effort, and with his last breath, he gasped, in a dying whisper, "Innocencia! Innocencia!"

On the afternoon of that day, any traveller passing by that wild bush-land would have noticed by the side of the road a newly-made grave, and above it a rough cross hastily formed of two stout saplings bound together with the wild vines of

CHAPTER XXX: TOO LATE.

the forest.

EPILOGUE: MEYER REAPPEARS.

On the 18th of August, 1863, there occurred in the ancient city of Magdeburg a great and important spectacle, and one that had long been expected by the scientific world of learned Germany.

It was a solemn and extraordinary meeting of all the effective, honorary, and corresponding members of the Entomological Society; attended also by numerous friends, learned savants, and ladies, all of whom had been assembled together in order to give a public reception and a hearty welcome home to one of the most distinguished members of the society, one of the most indefatigable investigators of the secrets of nature, an intrepid traveller who had been absent for years from his country, and who now returned from his many wanderings in the wilds of South America, where he had penetrated so far into the central regions that it had been impossible to follow his route even on the special maps and charts of the great collector, Simon Schropp.

Science appeared in full gala costume. All the members were in evening dress, and with many ladies in rich toilettes, they filled the vast saloon long before the hour of meeting, listening meanwhile to the strains of a band discoursing the 26th Sonata of Beethoven.

Suddenly a loud and enthusiastic cheer rent the air. "Meyer! Meyer! Hoch! Hoch! Meyer."

Necks were eagerly craned to catch the first glimpses of his arrival, handkerchiefs and hats were enthusiastically waved, and cheer after cheer welcomed the appearance of Meyer. As soon as the noise of the reception had calmed down, the president of the society arose, a president thin as a spit, and adorned with such flaming red hair that it gave him the aspect of an ember of fire.

"Yes!" he exclaimed, after swallowing a few drops of water to moisten his throat, "yes, here at last once more safe in the midst of us is the great and incomparable Wilhelm Tembel Meyer." Then in a long speech which lasted nearly two hours, and which was largely interlarded with most complimentary allusions to the prowess of the intrepid traveller, the speaker gave his auditors an outline of the course of the wanderings of, and the discoveries made by, their distinguished guest.

On the following day the newspapers of Madgeburg contained an extensive description of the festival and the speech of the president, and, as an appendage to the biographical notes relating to Meyer, they enumerated the entomological prodigies that he had collected in his many peregrinations.

"What is most worthy of admiration," said *Die Zeit*, "in all the immense collection that Dr. Meyer has gathered in his journeys, is without doubt a butterfly of a completely new genus and of a splendour beyond conception. It is the Papilio Innocentia." (Then followed a minute description, thoroughly German). "The name," added the paper, "given by the eminent naturalist to that superb specimen was in graceful homage to the beauty of a maiden of the deserts of the province of Mato Grosso (Brazil); a creature, according to the account of Dr. Meyer, of most enchanting loveliness. It is therefore seen that savants also have sensitive hearts, and sometimes can utilise science as a means to demonstrate sentiments which they are not generally supposed to possess."

Innocencia, poor girl! Alas! A few months only after the death of Cyrino her graceful form was delivered to Mother Earth, to sleep in the Sertão of Sant'Anna do Paranahyba, the last long sleep of Eternity.

Made in the USA
Coppell, TX
09 January 2024

27471345R00138